Kate Mosse is the author of six previous books, including the international bestseller *Labyrinth*. Translated into 38 languages and published in 40 countries, it also won the 2006 Richard & Judy Best Read award and was chosen as one of Waterstone's Top 25 novels of the past 25 years. The co-founder & honorary director of the Orange Prize for Fiction, Kate lives with her family in West Sussex and Carcassonne.

THE
WINTER
GHOSTS

Kate Mosse

An Orion paperback

First published in Great Britain in 2009
by Orion
This paperback edition published in 2010
by Orion Books Ltd,
Orion House, 5 Upper St Martin's Lane,
London WC2H 9EA

An Hachette UK company

7 9 10 8

A CIP catalogue record for this book
is available from the British Library
ISBN 978-1-4091-1799-5

Printed and bound in Great Britain
by Clays Ltd, St Ives plc

The Orion Publishing Group's policy is to use papers
that are natural, renewable and recyclable products and
made from wood grown in sustainable forests. The logging
and manufacturing processes are expected to conform to
the environmental regulations of the country of origin.

www.orionbooks.co.uk

'Known unto God'

RUDYARD KIPLING

*(epigraph carved on the tombstones raised
to the memory of unknown soldiers and airmen)*

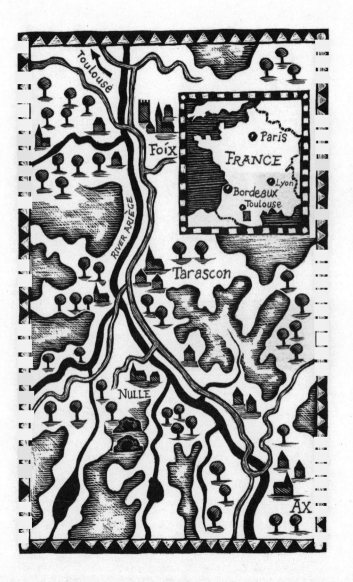

Contents

Lo Vièlh Ivèrn

Lo vièlh Ivèrn ambe sa samba ranca
Ara es tornat dins los nòstres camins
Le nèu retrais una flassada blanca
E'l Cerç bronzís dins las brancas dels pins.

Old Winter

Pitiful old Winter has returned,
Limping up and down our roads,
Spreading his white blanket of snow
While the Cers wind cries in the
    branches of the pine trees.

Traditional Occitan Song

TOULOUSE

April 1933

La Rue des Pénitents Gris

He walked like a man recently returned to the world. Every step was careful, deliberate. Every step to be relished.

He was tall and clean-shaven, a little thin perhaps. Dressed by Savile Row. A light woollen suit of herringbone weave, the jacket wide on the shoulders and narrow at the waist. His fawn gloves matched his trilby. He looked like an Englishman, secure in his right to be on such a street on such a pleasant afternoon in spring.

But nothing is as it seems.

For every step was a little too careful, a little too deliberate, as if he was unwilling to take even the ground beneath his feet entirely for granted. And as he walked, his clever, quick eyes darted from side to side, as if he were determined to record every tiny detail.

Toulouse was considered one of the most beautiful cities in the south of France. Certainly, Freddie admired it. The elegance of its nineteenth-century buildings, the medieval past that slept beneath the pavements and colonnades, the bell towers and cloisters of Saint-Etienne, the bold river dividing the city in two. The pink brick facades, blushing in the April sunshine, gave Toulouse its affectionate nickname, *la ville rose*. Little had changed since Freddie had last visited, at the tail end of the 1920s. He had been another man then, a tattered man, worn threadbare by grief.

Things were different now.

In his right hand, Freddie carried directions scribbled on the back of a napkin from Bibent, where he'd lunched on filet mignon and a blowsy Bordeaux. In his left-hand breast pocket was a letter patterned with antiquity and dust, secure in a pasteboard wallet. It was this – and the fact that, at last, he had the opportunity to return – which brought him back to Toulouse today. The mountains where he'd come across the document held a strong significance for him, and though he had never read the letter, it was a precious possession.

Freddie crossed the Place du Capitole, heading towards the cathedral of Saint-Sernin. He walked through a network of small streets, obtuse little alleyways filled with jazz bars and poetry cellars and gloomy restaurants. He sidestepped couples on the pavements, lovers and families and friends out enjoying the warm afternoon. He passed through tiny squares and hidden *ruelles*, and along the rue du Taur, until he reached the street he was looking for. Freddie hesitated at the corner, as if having second thoughts. Then he continued on, walking briskly now, dragging his shadow behind him.

Halfway along the rue des Pénitents Gris was a *librairie* and antiquarian bookseller. His destination. He stopped dead to read the name of the proprietor painted in black lettering above the door. Momentarily, his silhouette was imprinted on the building. Then he shifted position and the window was once more flooded with gentle sunlight, causing the metal grille to glint.

Freddie stared at the display for a moment, at the antique volumes embossed with gold leaf, and the highly polished leather slip casings of black and red, at the ridged spines of works by Montaigne and Anatole France and Maupassant. Other, less familiar names, too: Antonin Gadal and Félix Garrigou; and volumes of ghost stories by Blackwood and James and Sheridan Le Fanu.

'Now or never,' he said.

The old-fashioned handle was stiff and the door dug in its heels as Freddie pushed it open. A brass bell rattled somewhere distant at the back of the shop. The coarse rush matting sighed beneath the soles of his shoes as he stepped in.

'*Il y a quelqu'un?*' he said in clipped French. 'Anybody about?'

The contrast between the brightness outside and the patchwork of shadows within made Freddie blink. But there was a pleasing smell of dust and afternoons, glue and paper and polished wooden shelves. Particles of dust danced in and out of the beams of slatted sunlight. He was sure now that he had come to the right place and he felt something unwind inside him. Relief that he had finally made it here, perhaps, or of being at his journey's end.

Freddie took off his hat and gloves and placed them on the long wooden counter. Then he reached into the pocket of his suit jacket and brought out the small pasteboard wallet.

'Hello?' he called a second time. 'Monsieur Saurat?'

He heard footsteps, then the creak of a small door at the back of the shop, and a man walked through. Freddie's first impression was of flesh; rolls of skin at

[6]

the neck and wrists, a smooth and unlined face beneath a shock of white hair. He did not, in any way, look like the medieval scholar Freddie was expecting.

'Monsieur Saurat?'

The man nodded. Cautious, bored, uninterested in a casual caller.

'I need help with a translation,' Freddie said. 'I was told you might be the man for such a job.'

Keeping his eyes on Saurat, Freddie carefully slipped the letter from its casing. It was a heavy weave, the colour of dirty chalk, not paper at all, but something far older. The handwriting was uneven and scratched.

Saurat let his gaze slip to it. Freddie watched his eyes sharpen, first with surprise, then astonishment. Then greed.

'May I?'

'Be my guest.'

Taking a pair of half-moon spectacles from his top pocket, Saurat perched them on the end of his nose. He produced a pair of thin, linen gloves from beneath the counter, pulled them on. Holding the letter gently at the corner between forefinger and thumb, he held it up to the light.

'Parchment. Probably late medieval.'

'Quite right.'

'Written in Occitan, the old language of this region.'

'Yes.' All this Freddie knew.

Saurat gave him a hard look, then dropped his eyes back to the letter. An intake of breath, then he began to read the opening lines aloud. His voice was surprisingly light.

'*Bones and shadows and dust. I am the last. The others have slipped away into darkness. Around me now, at the end of my days, only an echo in the still air of the memory of those who once I loved. Solitude, silence. Peyre sant . . .*'

Saurat stopped and stared now with interest at the reserved Englishman standing before him. He did not look like a collector, but then one never could tell.

He cleared his throat. 'May I ask where you came by this, Monsieur . . . ?'

'Watson.' Freddie took his card from his pocket and laid it with a snap on the counter between them. 'Frederick Watson.'

'You are aware this is a document of some historical significance?'

'To me its significance is purely personal.'

'That may be, but nevertheless . . .' Saurat shrugged.

'It is something that has been in your family for some time?'

Freddie hesitated. 'Is there a place we could talk?'

'Of course.' Saurat gestured to a low card table and four leather armchairs set in an alcove at the rear of the shop. 'Please.'

Freddie took the letter and sat down, watching as Saurat stooped beneath the counter again, this time producing two thick glass tumblers and a bottle of mellow, golden brandy. He was unusually graceful, delicate even, Freddie thought, for such a large man. Saurat poured them both a generous measure, then lowered himself into the chair opposite. The leather sighed beneath his weight.

'So, will you translate it for me?'

'Of course. But I am still intrigued to know how you come to be in possession of such a document.'

'It's a long story.'

Another shrug. 'I have the time.'

Freddie leaned forward and slowly fanned his long fingers across the surface of the table, making patterns on the green baize.

'Tell me, Saurat, do you believe in ghosts?'

A smile stole across the other man's lips.

'I am listening.'

Freddie breathed out, with relief or some other emotion, it was hard to tell.

'Well then,' he said, settling back in his chair. 'The story begins almost five years ago, not so very far from here.'

ARIÈGE

December 1928

Tarascon-sur-Ariège

It was a dirty night in late November, a few days shy of my twenty-seventh birthday, when I boarded the boat train for Calais.

I had no ties to keep me in England, and my health in those days was poor. I'd spent some time in a sanatorium and, since then, had struggled to find a vocation, a calling in life. A stint as a junior assistant in an ecclesiastical architect's office, a month as a commission agent; nothing had stuck. I was not suited to work nor it, apparently, to me. After a particularly vicious bout of influenza, my doctor suggested a tour of the castles and ruins of the Ariège would do my shattered nerves some good. The clean air of the mountains might restore me, he said, where all else had failed.

So I set off, with no particular route in mind. I

was no more lonely motoring on the Continent than I had been in England, surrounded by acquaintances and my few remaining friends who didn't understand why I could not forget. A decade had passed since the Armistice. Besides, there was nothing unique to my suffering. Every family had lost someone in the War: fathers and uncles, sons, husbands and brothers. Life moved on.

But not for me. As each green summer slipped into the copper and gold of another autumn, I became less able, not more, to accept my brother's death. Less willing to believe George was gone. And although I went through all the appropriate emotions – disbelief, denial, anger, regret – grief still held me in its grasp. I despised the wretched creature I had become, but seemed unable to do anything about it. Looking back, I am not certain that, when I stood on the rocking boat watching the white cliffs of Dover growing smaller behind me, I had any intention of returning.

The change of scene did help, though. Once I'd negotiated my way through those northern towns and villages where the scent of battle still hung heavy in the air, I felt less stuck in the past than I had at home. Here in France, I was a stranger. I was not supposed to fit in and nor did anyone expect me to.

No one knew me and I knew no one. There was nobody to disappoint. And while I cannot say that I took much pleasure in my surroundings, certainly the day-to-day business of eating and driving and finding a bed occupied my waking hours.

The night, of course, was another matter.

So it was that some few weeks later, on 15 December, I arrived at Tarascon-sur-Ariège in the foothills of the Pyrenees. It was late in the afternoon and I was stiff from rattling over the basic mountain roads. The temperature inside my little box saloon was barely higher than that outside. My breath had caused the windows to steam up, and I was obliged to wipe the condensation from the windscreen with my sleeve.

I entered the small town via the avenue de Foix in the pink light of the fading day. The sun falls early in those high valleys and the shadows on the narrow cobbled streets were already deep. Ahead of me, a thin, eighteenth-century clock tower perched high on a vertiginous outcrop, like a sentinel to welcome home the solitary traveller. Straight away, there was something about the place – a sense of confidence and acceptance of its place in the world – that appealed to me. A suggestion of old values coexisting with the demands of the twentieth century.

Through the gaps between the window and the frame of the car slipped the acrid yet sweet smell of burning wood and resin. I saw flickering lights in little houses, waiters in long black aprons moving between tables in a café, and I ached to be part of that world.

I decided to stop for the night. At the junction with the Pont Vieux, I was obliged suddenly to brake to avoid a man on a bicycle. The beam from his lamp jumped and lurched as he swerved the potholes in the road. While I waited for him to pass, my eye was drawn by the bright light of the *boulangerie* window opposite. As I watched, a young sales assistant, her coarse brown hair escaping from beneath her cap, reached down into the glass cabinet and lifted out a *Jésuite*, or perhaps a cream *éclair*.

Much time has passed and memory is an unreliable friend, but, in my mind's eye, still I see her pause for a moment, then smile shyly at me before placing the *pâtisserie* in the box and tying it with ribbon. The thinnest shaft of light entered the empty chambers of my heart, just for a moment. Then it disappeared, extinguished by the weight of all that had gone before.

I found lodgings without difficulty at the Grand Hôtel de la Poste, which advertised a garage for the use of its customers. Although my yellow Austin

Seven was the sole occupant, there was a service station, the Garage Fontez, a little further along the street and the sense that things in Tarascon were on the up. This was confirmed as I signed the register. The hotel proprietor told me how an aluminium factory had opened only a few weeks before. It would, he believed, bring prosperity to the district and give the young men a reason to stay.

The precise details of the conversation escape me now. At that time, I'd lost the appetite for casual talk. Over ten years of mourning, my ability to engage with anyone other than George had ebbed away. He walked beside me and was the only person to whom I could unburden myself. I needed no one else.

But on that December afternoon in that little hotel, I saw a glimpse of how other people lived, and regretted I could not learn to do the same. Even now I remember the *patron*'s passion for the project of regeneration, his optimism and ambition for his town. It stood in stark contrast to my own limited horizons. As always at such moments, I felt more of an outsider than ever. I was glad when, having shown me to my lodgings, he left me alone.

The room was on the first floor, overlooking the street, with a pleasant enough outlook. A large window with freshly painted shutters, a single bed with heavy counterpane, a washstand and an armchair. Plain, clean, anonymous. The sheets were cold to the touch. We suited one another, the room and I.

La Tour du Castella

I unpacked, washed the dirt of the road from my face and hands, then sat and looked down on the avenue de Foix as I smoked a cigarette.

I decided to take a turn around the town on foot before dinner. It was still early, but the temperature had fallen, and the cobblers and *pharmacie*, the *boucherie* and the *mercerie* had already turned off their lights and fastened their shutters. A row of dead men's eyes, seeing nothing, revealing nothing.

I walked along the quai de l'Ariège, back to the stone bridge over the river, at the point where the white waters of the Ariège and the Vicdessos meet. I loitered a while in the dusk, then continued over to the right bank of the river. This, I had been told, was the oldest and most distinctive part of the town, the *quartier* Mazel-Viel.

I strolled through a pretty garden, bleak in winter, which perfectly matched my mood. I paused, as I always did, at the memorial raised in honour of those who had fallen on the battlefields of Ypres and Mons and Verdun. Even in Tarascon, far from the theatre of war, there were so many names set down in stone. So very many names.

Just behind the monument, a corridor of gaunt fir and black pine led to the wrought-iron gate of the cemetery. The stone tips of carved angels' wings, Christian crosses and the peaks of one or two more elaborate tombs were just visible above the high walls. I hesitated, tempted to visit the sleepers in the damp earth, but resisted the impulse. I knew better than to linger among the dead. I started to turn away.

But I was too slow. I saw him. For a fraction of a second, a shadow in the diminishing light or a trick of my unreliable eyes, I saw him standing on the shallow old stone steps directly ahead of me. I felt a jolt of happiness and raised my hand to wave. Like the old days.

'George?'

His name dropped into the silent air. Then I felt my ribs tighten a notch, cracking like the tired winding mechanism on our old grandfather clock, and my arm fell back to my side in despair.

There was nobody there. There never would be.

I pushed my hands deep into the pockets of my overcoat as the bell in the *cloche-mur* struck four, the notes echoing away into nothing in the damp air. In those days, the truth was that though I feared to see him, I grieved when he did not come. And when he did, I felt a rush of joy, elation, and for a moment was able to believe he was still alive. That it had all been a stupid mistake.

Then I would remember and my haggard heart would fold in upon itself once more.

'George,' I whispered, knowing there would be no answer.

I slumped down on the ledge of the memorial. As I leaned against the stone for support, I was conscious of the names of the dead pressing against my back as if they were engraving themselves on my skin.

The familiar image of a photograph slipped into my mind. Once it had sat on the sideboard at home in a tortoiseshell frame. Now I carried it loose in the bottom of my suitcase. Taken in September 1914, it was fixed in the sepia tones of the past. Mother sat in the centre of the photograph, beautiful and remote in her high-necked blouse and brooch. Standing behind her, Father on one side and George on the other, proud in his uniform. The garter badge and Roussillon plume gleamed on his cap. Captain George Watson, Royal Sussex Regiment, 39th Division.

I am sitting a little apart from the tableau, an awkward adolescent of thirteen. My hair is lying not quite flat. At the moment the shutter clicked, something made me turn away from the camera and towards George. Over the years I have examined and re-examined the photograph, trying to read the expression in my eyes. Is it his reassurance I am seeking, his admiration? Or is it rather a child's impotent anger at being made to collude in such a charade? I don't know. However many times I stare at that dusty, captured moment and try to remember what was going through my mind, I can't.

Two days later, George was sent to join the 13th Battalion in France. I do recall how proud Father was, how boastful Mother, and how full of dread was I. Crippling, overpowering dread. Even then, I knew that road would not lead to glory.

How long did I sit there on that cold winter seat in Tarascon, the chill seeping through the heavy fabric of my coat and tweeds? Time stretches and shrinks, does not stay fixed when we most need it to. I thought of my parents, distant and uninterested. Of George, of all those who had died, becoming less defined as the years went by. The simple truth was that I was burdened by my life and the fact of George's death.

With hindsight, I see that all these emotions assaulted me simultaneously. Delusion and hope and longing, all tumbling one after the other like a falling line of dominoes. It was, after all, a path well-worn. A decade of mourning leaves its footprints on the heart.

Finally, I pulled myself together and moved on, grateful for the darkness. I stopped a while at the church and attempted to decipher the handwritten notice set outside on the wall, forcing myself to concentrate on the words. It appeared that the name – La Daurade – was derived from '*daurado*' in the local language, which meant 'golden one' or 'gilded one', and referred to a statue of the Virgin that had once been housed within the church. I tried to ignite a spark of interest, if nothing else out of respect for my previous, short-lived employment in a firm of ecclesiastical architects. But in truth, I felt nothing. And my thoughts insisted on spiralling back to the dead sleeping in the cold earth. Shattered bones and mud and blood. The headstones and the graves, the wild and untended places between.

I shook my head. I didn't want to be haunted by images of George's final hours, of barbed wire, limbs tangled and trapped and torn. I did not want to hear the crump of the guns or the screams of men and horses brought down in a hail of bullets or a cloud of gas or the sudden wrenching away of the ground beneath their feet.

The trouble was that I knew both too much and too little. After ten years of trying to find out what had happened to George in 1916, I had armed myself only with possibilities of what might have been. Rather than helping me to accept and to move on, that ugly, violent knowledge had been the undoing of me.

Again, I tried to think about other things. I looked up at the beauty of the church, the pleasing symmetry and gentle detail of stone, and I wished, as I had so often before, that these fragments of history had the power to move me as once they had. My fingers, stiff in my leather gloves, slipped to the Penguin score of Bach's Brandenburg Concerto No. 3 in the pocket of my coat. An investment of two shillings and sixpence, this, too, an attempt to remind me of what I had once valued so highly. But music, like everything else, had lost its charm. I was no longer moved by Vaughan Williams's soaring cadenzas or

Elgar's falling sevenths, any more than I was by the sight of white apple blossom in March, or the vivid yellow of broom in the hedgerows in April, or a haze of bluebells in a wood in May. Nothing touched me. Everything had ceased to matter on the day the telegram arrived: MISSING IN ACTION. PRESUMED DEAD.

I continued my solitary circuit, walking through the place des Consuls, careless of the cold that made my ears ache. There was the occasional rattle of a plate or a cup from behind shuttered windows, the intermittent burst of conversation or the crackle of a wireless. But mostly I was alone, with only the sound of my boots on the cobbled stones for company.

I followed the winding steps through the old quarter and climbed up to the foot of the Tour du Castella, the thin tower I'd noticed when I drove into Tarascon. From this vantage point, I could see the timeless peaks of the Pyrenees surrounding the town like a ring of stone. On the horizon was the summit of the Roc de Sédour, the snow on its peak a ghostly white against the black sky. To the south, the river gorge of the Vicdessos.

In the *quartier* Saint-Roch, the lights from the Chateau Piquemal sparkled like the illuminations on the pier at Bognor Regis. The avenue de Sabart was lined with allotments and *cabanes* for the market gardeners, jostling for position with the houses that had sprung up like weeds in the *quartier* de la Gare. And in the mouth of the southern tip of the valley, the new factory buildings sat long and flat and squat, modern gatekeepers to the older rhythms of the mountains, reminding me of the greenhouses in the walled garden at my childhood home.

Clouds of white smoke belched from the chimneys, shot through with eerie blue or green or yellow tints from the metals they consumed. Aluminium, cobalt, copper. And in the air the smell of burning, the scent of industry. Of time marching on.

It was not possible to get inside the Tour du Castella. A small door was nailed shut, and halfway up was a blind window with a black grille across it. The weeds grew wild around the base. The grey stone was covered with moss and lichen.

Its position was vertiginous enough, though. The ground surrounding it dropped sharply away. There was no barrier or handrail, nothing to stop the intrepid traveller who had climbed this far from slipping or stepping out.

As I looked down, I felt suddenly dizzy, from the cold, the narrowness of the ledge around the foot of the tower. The vast sense of space and dusk. For an instant, I thought of how easy it would be to finish things now. To close my eyes and step out into the gentle sky. Feel nothing but air as I fell down, down into the foaming waters of the Ariège below. I thought of the revolver in my portmanteau, hidden beneath my Fair Isle slipover, a match to George's old service Webley that I'd not been able to bring myself to use.

I had acquired the weapon in a rare moment of purpose six years ago, just before the mental collapse that had seen me confined for some months to a sanatorium. Hurrying down a Dickensian alley in the East End of London that was black with soot, the air rank with resignation, I'd made my way to an address slipped to me by one of George's fellow officers. Simpson was a ruin of a man, drinking himself to death to escape the shame of being the only one to have made it back. So he understood, better than most, the importance of a quick and easy solution to things should the burden of living become too much. I bought that particular revolver knowing George had owned one, and, for a while, the possession of it had given me courage. But I'd funked it. I had never fired the gun. Never even loaded it.

At that instant, standing at the foot of the tower on the top of the precipitous hill in Tarascon, I felt a rush of blood to the head at the thought that perhaps the moment finally had come. Elation at the possibility of decisive action. Of joining George. But only for an instant. Then, as at every other time, the impulse slunk away with its tail between its legs. I stepped back from the ledge. Felt the safety of the stone at my back, my hands flat against the brick.

A few minutes passed until my head stopped spinning. Then I turned and descended the wide, shallow steps that led down from the mound to the streets below. Was it courage or cowardice that stopped me? Still I cannot say. Even now, I find it hard to tell those impostors one from the other.

*

Later, after a modest dinner in the restaurant opposite the hotel, unwilling to be alone with my thoughts, I sought out a bar in the Faubourg Sainte-Quitterie where men were prepared to accept without question a stranger into their company.

Their rough voices spoke with pride of the future of Tarascon. And as I raised a glass to the prosperity of the town, I did understand this need to move forward, to forget. How, with drums and penny whistles, the world marched on. Such swaggering industry boasted to travellers and citizens alike that there was a future there for the taking, not just tawdry memories. That the ruined landscapes of Flanders should be allowed to fade from memory. Honour the dead, yes. Remember, yes, but fare forward. Look to tomorrow. Jazz and girls with bobbed hair and those chic, false new buildings in Piccadilly. Pretend that it had all been worth it.

As the evening staggered on in a haze of red wine and strong tobacco, I have a recollection that I tried to tell my drinking companions how, in ten years, I had not learned to forget. How electric signs and teeming carriageways could not drown out the voices of those who had been lost. How the beloved dead were always there, glimpsed out of the corner of the eye. At one's side.

But my schoolboy French meant they were spared my philosophising and besides, for all its rituals, grief is a solitary business. So the evening ended with the shaking of hands, the slap on the back. Companionship, certainly, but precious little communication.

When finally I found my bed, I was restless and

wakeful. The tolling of the single bell marked the passing hours of the night. Not until the pale dawn crept through the wooden slats of the shutters did I, at last, fall into a deep and heavy sleep.

I tell you about that evening in such detail, Saurat, not because I cared so very much about this particular town. It could have been any one of a hundred places in that corner of southern France. But it is important to recount every ordinary minute so you understand that nothing about that night in Tarascon could be seen as the harbinger of what was to come. I staggered between remembrance and maudlin self-pity, which was how it was in those days. On other nights, things had been worse, and they had been better. I occupied an emotional no-man's-land, neither moving forward, nor moving back.

But although I did not yet know it, the watcher in the hills had me in her sights. She was already there. Waiting, for me.

On The Mountain Road to Vicdessos

In the darkest days of my confinement in the sanatorium, then during my convalescence at home in Sussex, dawn was the part of the day I dreaded most. It was in those early hours that the barrenness of my existence seemed most starkly at odds with the waking world around me. The blue of the sky, the silver underside of the leaves on trees coming back to life in the spring, celandine and cow parsley in the hedgerows, all appeared to mock my dull spirits.

Looking back, the reason for my breakdown was perfectly straightforward, though it did not seem so at the time. To those around me, to my parents certainly, it was peculiar – in bad taste, almost – to have waited so long before going to pieces. It was not until six years after George's death that my battered mind gave up the fight, though in truth it had been a steady deterioration.

We were at a restaurant not far from Fortnum & Mason's to celebrate my twenty-first birthday. I can still remember the taste of the Montebello 1915 champagne on my tongue, the same vintage, as it happens, Fortnum's had provided for the Everest expedition that year. But as we sat there in a brittle silence, Father and Mother and I, George was a shadow at our table. It was his presence that had made us a family. He had been the glue. Without him, we were three strangers with nothing to say. And here I was, the other son, sipping champagne and opening gifts, when George had never even reached his majority. It was wrong.

All wrong.

Was I the elder brother now, having lived longer than George? Had we exchanged places? Such thoughts, becoming ever more heated, spun round and round in my mind. The waiters glided past us in black and white. The bubbles of the champagne scratched at the back of my throat. The clatter of cutlery grated on my nerves.

'Do make an effort, Frederick,' my mother snapped. 'Do at least pretend to be enjoying yourself, even if you are not.'

'Leave the boy alone,' my father growled, but he

waved away the offer of a second bottle of Monte-bello.

All I could think about were birthdays past, when George had made me laugh and brought me presents and transformed an ordinary day into something special. A red and white top when I was five. A bow and arrow at nine. His final gift to me, a first edition of Captain Scott's *The Voyage of the Discovery Vol I*, with its blue embossed board cover, sent from France in December 1915, tied up in brown paper and string.

That was it. The memory of that book. Having fought the truth of his death for six years, I gave in. There, in that plush and velvet restaurant, my mind came undone. Everything started to unravel. I remember how I put down my champagne flute carefully, deliberately, on the table in front of me, but after that, almost nothing. Did I weep? Did I disturb the fossil-ised ladies and military veterans by raising my voice or rolling my eyes? By breaking the porcelain or some other such pantomime? I can't recall. Just the com-forting haze of the morphine and the snow falling on London and the rattling journey by car as I was taken from Piccadilly to a private hospital outside Midhurst.

In the sanatorium, Christmas and the New Year of 1923 came and went without me. Only when spring came and the mistle thrush outside my window began its fluty song, did the world shyly come back into focus. An hour a day, walking up and down in the airing court accompanied by two starched nurses, then only one. Then, outings that lasted a little longer and were undertaken alone, until, at the end of April, the doctors considered I was strong enough to be released into my family's care.

I was sent home. Father was ashamed of my lack of backbone, and was rarely there. Mother was no more interested in me now I was an invalid than she had been prior to my collapse. These days, I understand where her antipathy originated. I feel some pity for her. Having provided my father with a son, she had found herself obliged to go through the whole business again five years later when she'd thought all that kind of thing was over. At the time, when I was growing up, I just took it as read that there was something unlikeable about me and tried not to care too much about it.

Nonetheless, during the summer and autumn of that year, I recovered. But each tiny improvement in my health took me further from George, and in truth, his remained the only company I wished for. It felt like a betrayal to learn to live without him.

Life went on at its steady pace. The shadow cast by the War grew weaker. All those months and years, sliding by, one much like the other. And still, despair at the break of another dawn. Each morning, as light gave back shape to the futile world, a stark reminder of how much I had lost.

But in the Grand Hôtel de la Poste in Tarascon, at the fag end of 1928, I woke at ten o'clock, having slept right through the early-morning horrors, and without a weight pressing down upon my chest. I flexed my fingers, my shoulders, my arms, feeling them as a part of me, not something separate. Not something dead.

Again it is possible that it is only with hindsight that my thawing emotions are evident. Or that, having stepped back from the edge that previous evening, I see there had been some significant change in me. But I want to remember that I rose from my bed with a certain energy. Outside in the street, I could hear a girl singing. A folk song, or some tune of the mountains, which touched me by its simplicity. I flung wide the shutters, experiencing the snap of cold air on my arms, and felt, if not precisely happy, then at least not unhappy.

Did I smile down at the girl? Or did she, aware of

my scrutiny, look up at me? I cannot recall, only that the old-fashioned melody seemed to hang heavy in the air long after she had stopped singing.

I was the sole occupant of the dining room. A plain woman served me warm white rolls and ham, with fresh butter and a coarse plum jam that was somehow both sweet and sour. There was coffee, too; real beans, not chicory ground with barley and malt. I had an appetite and ate with pleasure, not solely for the purpose of keeping body and soul together. I took my time with my pipe, filling the *salle à manger* with clouds of smoke that danced in the December light, and was tempted to stay another night. In the end, a certain restiveness within me demanded I keep moving.

It was a little after eleven by the time I had settled my bill, retrieved my Austin from the garage and put Tarascon behind me. I headed south towards Vicdessos. I had no particular destination in mind and was content to see where the road took me. My Baedeker recommended sites with splendid caves at Niaux and Lombrives. It was hardly likely they would be open to visitors in December, but I felt a stab of interest nonetheless. Enough, at least, to make me journey that way.

I followed the line of the river through a magnificent, archaic landscape. Mostly, I had the road to myself. I saw a wooden cart drawn by oxen, then an old military truck rumbled past. Its engine wheezed, its green tarpaulin roof was ragged, splattered by mud, and one of its headlamps was missing. An old warhorse, not yet put out to grass.

The mercury was falling but there was no snow, although the higher I drove, the heavier the canopy of frost that covered the plains. But I could imagine that if one came this way in late summer, there would be fields of yellow sunflowers and olive trees with their silver-green leaves and black fruit. On the terraces of the few houses scattered on the sharp hillsides, I could picture earth-coloured pots filled with white and pink geraniums the size of a man's hand, and vines of red and green grapes ripening in the noonday sun. Twice I pulled over and got out to stretch my legs and smoke a cigarette, before continuing on.

The lush winter beauty of the river valleys of the Ariège, through which I had motored the previous day, here yielded to a more prehistoric landscape of caves and plunging cliffs. The rock and forest came right down to the road, as though seeking to reclaim what had been taken from it by man. The clouds seem to hang suspended between the mountains, like smoke from an autumn bonfire, and so low that I felt as if I could reach out and touch them. On every peak was a limestone outcrop that drew the eye. But rather than the romantic, crumbling chateaux or the remains of a long-deserted military strongholds I had seen in Limoux and Couiza, here were jagged clefts in the mountain face. Not the echoes of habitation, but something more primitive.

My mind was alive with memories of my classroom at prep school. Chalk dust and the yellow light of an October afternoon, listening to the master tell the bloodstained story of these borderlands between France and Spain. Of how, in the thirteenth century, the Catholic Church had waged war against the Albigensians. A civil war, a war of attrition that lasted more than a hundred years. Burnings and torture and systematic persecution, giving birth to the Inquisition. And to us boys of ten and eleven, who had not seen death, did not yet know what war meant, it was the stuff of adventure. The sunlit days of childhood, nothing fractured, nothing spoiled.

Later, a little older, the same master's voice, telling of the sixteenth-century battles of religion between the Catholics and the Huguenots. A green land, he called the Languedoc. A green land soaked red with the blood of the faithful.

And in our times, too. Even if this corner of France had suffered less than the Pas de Calais, than all the ravaged villages and woods of the north-east, the war memorials at every crossroads, the cemeteries and plaques, told the same story. Everywhere, evidence of men dying before their time.

I pulled over and killed the engine. My fragile good spirits scattered in an instant, replaced by familiar symptoms. Damp palms, dry throat, the familiar spike of pain in my stomach. I took off my cap and leather gloves, ran my fingers through my hair and covered my eyes. Sticky fingers smelling of hair oil and shame, that grief should still come so easily, that after all the talking cures, the treatments and kindness, the kneeling at hard wooden pews at evensong, I still carried within me a cracked heart that refused to heal.

It was then that I first became aware of a disturbance in the air. A kind of restlessness. I looked sharply up through the smeared windscreen, but saw nothing out of the ordinary. The road was deserted. No one had passed by on either side for some time.

Yet there was a suggestion of movement nonetheless, a shifting of light on the ridges high above. The mountains loomed more menacingly over me and the hillside appeared even closer, those ancient forests of evergreen and the naked, unforgiving branches of trees in winter. What secrets did they contain within their shadows?

My heart skipped a beat. I wound down the window. The silence surged around me. Again, nothing. No telltale footsteps or voices or rumbling wheels in the distance. Only later, when it was over, did it occur to me that the silence was peculiar. I *should* have been able to hear something. The roar of the furnaces back in Tarascon or the belching chimneys of the factories at my back. The sound of metal on metal or the song of the railway lines snaking up through the Haute Vallée. The rapids on the river. But I was aware only of the silence. Silence, as if I were the only man left alive in the world.

Then I heard it. No, not heard. I *sensed* it. A whispering, almost like singing.

'*The others have slipped away into darkness.*'

I caught my breath.

'Who's there?'

I often heard the ghost of George's voice inside

my head, though it was growing fainter with the passing years. But this was different. It was a lighter sound, gentle and exquisite, carried on the cold air. A reverberation, an echo of words once spoken in this place? Or the girl I'd heard singing outside the hotel in Tarascon, her plaintive melody somehow reaching high into the mountains? Or was that too fanciful? Of course there was nobody there, no one at all. How could there be?

I realised my hands were clamped rigidly to the steering wheel. The temperature had fallen and what looked to be snow clouds were approaching from the south. It was bitterly cold inside the car, too. I wound up the window, flexed my fingers until they were in working order and tucked my scarf tightly into the neck of my jumper.

I took refuge from my troubling thoughts in practical things. Leaning over, I studied the map book and tried to work out where, precisely, I was. I'd been heading towards Vicdessos, which was about fifteen miles from Tarascon. My intention had been to turn there and head across country on the back road to Ax-les-Thermes. Two chaps from home were at the resort for a week's skiing and had invited me to join them for Christmas. I'd neither accepted nor declined the invitation, but now saw some merit in being among friends. I'd been driving around on my own for a few weeks now and the companionship might do me good.

I peered outside. If the map was accurate, it appeared I had missed the turning to Ax-les-Thermes. And if the weather were changing for the worse, it would be lunacy to head higher into the mountains. The sun was covered completely now and the sky was the colour of dirty linen. Far better to rejoin the main road.

I traced the route with my finger. If my calculations were correct, I could continue this way for another mile or two, past the villages of Aliat, Lapège and Capoulet-et-Junac, then I'd find myself back on the road to Vicdessos on the far side of this low range of hills.

Leaving the map book open on the passenger seat, I put my gloves back on and fired the electric starter. The little saloon spluttered back into life and I drove on.

The Storm Hits

I had gone no more than a mile or so when a flurry of sleet splattered against the windscreen. I turned on the wiper, which only smeared muck and ice over the glass. Winding down my side window, I reached round and tried to clear the worst of it with my handkerchief.

A violent gust of wind hit the Austin head on. I dropped from third to second gear, acutely aware that the tyres would not hold if the sleet turned to ice. A single snowflake, as large as a sixpence, settled upon the bonnet, then another and another. Within seconds, or so it seemed, I was in the centre of a blizzard. The snow was swirling and twisting in the spiralling draught, settling on the roof of the car and deadening the sound inside.

Then I heard what sounded like a rumble of thunder,

echoing through the space between the mountains. Was that likely, thunder and snow at one and the same time? Even possible? As I considered it, a second roll reverberated through the valley, making the question obsolete.

I pressed on, inch by inch. The road seemed to be getting narrower. To one side, the great, grey walls of the mountains; to the other, an abrupt chasm, the forested hillside dropping sharply away. Another growl of thunder then a snap of lightning, silhouetting the trees black against an electric sky.

I switched on my headlamps, feeling the tyres struggling to keep a grip on the steep, slippery road, as on we lurched into the spiteful headwind. And always the shriek of the wiper, struggling back and forth, back and forth.

The windscreen had fugged up. My nose itched with the smell of damp wool and leather, of petrol fumes, of the damp carpet beneath my feet. I leaned forward and wiped the inside of the windscreen with my sleeve again. It made no difference.

I knew I had to find shelter, but there were no houses to be seen, no signs of human habitation at all, not even a solitary shepherd's hut. Just an endless expanse of cold silence.

Another childhood memory seeped into my mind. The old attic nursery, the night lights burnt out. Me crying in the dark, jolted awake by bad dreams and calling out for a mother who never came. Then George, sitting at the end of my bed, opening the curtains to let the silver moon in, saying there was nothing to be afraid of. How nothing could harm me. How we were the Watson boys, invincible and courageous. Nothing could get us so long as we stuck together. And with George by my side, I believed it.

How old must he have been? Eleven, twelve? And how was it that he knew how to comfort a lonely boy who was scared of the dark – neither showing too much sympathy, nor too little – and understood that he should never mention it again.

'The Watson boys,' I murmured.

So I talked to myself to keep my spirits up. I was in no actual, physical danger, I said. It was just a matter of holding one's nerve. The odds against the car being struck by lightning were small. Too many tall trees around. The storm sounded worse than it was, and as for the thunder? A by-product of the unusual weather, no more. There was nothing to be afraid of. Noise could not hurt, noise could not kill. Not as bullets did, not as chlorine gas, not as bombs or bayonets. George had known what he faced every moment of every day. This was nothing to what he, to what all of them, had coped with.

I kept it up, but the comparisons rang hollow in my head. Courage hadn't saved George in the end, hadn't saved any of them. If the weather deteriorated further, the road would quickly become impassable. The danger was real, not just a shadow in the dark. The surface was already turning to ice. It would be easy to lose control and plunge over the edge.

Or, if not a crash, then the cold could get me. Cold could defeat even the strongest of men. Franklin in the Arctic, Wilson and Bowers in the Antarctic, Mallory and Irvine lost on Everest. Like Scott, my boyhood hero, I would die stranded in a stark, un-forgiving world. Unlike Scott, eleven days from base camp, nobody would come looking for me. Nobody knew where I was.

As I debated my situation, I became more aware of its irony. Here I was, facing the oblivion I'd flirted with the previous evening at the Tour du Castella. Yet less then twenty-four hours later, when fate itself stepped in to give me a hand, I no longer wanted to die.

'I do not want to die.'

I said it aloud, surprising myself, and was astounded to discover it was true. Then another snap of lighting struck directly in front of me, illuminating a wooden signpost at the side of the road.

Like an idiot, I pulled at the handbrake. The front wheels locked. Fighting to keep control, I dragged down on the steering wheel, but too hard. I felt the tyres go from under me. I was skidding sideways, hurtling towards the sheer drop. Closer, closer towards the void. Then there was a sharp crack. I jerked at the wheel again, pulling down in the opposite direction, twisting the Austin 180 degrees. In that split second, I remember wondering how it was going to end.

Something on the underbelly of the car impaled itself like an anchor in the ragged surface of the road. It slowed me down, but it was not enough. I had too much forward momentum. I was still rushing towards the precipice.

This was it.

I threw up my hands. Felt the engine cut out, then a thud, and glass showered into my lap. Everything slowed, movement, momentum, sound. Fragments of life flashed, yes, into my mind and out. Broken images of my parents, snapshots of the girls I had tried to love. The way the November light struck the plaque commemorating the dead of the Royal Sussex Regiment in the chapel in Chichester Cathedral. Memories of George.

And I wondered if he had seen death, like a shadow, coming to meet him? Had he recognised the moment for what it was? Looking back, I am astonished at how these thoughts came, so gentle and so quiet, into my mind. No more panic or fear, only peace. I had the sensation of the light dimming and a downy softness, like black feathers, and I hoped that George had felt this obscure pleasure at the moment of his departing. No terror, most of all no pain. Just release. The sense of being welcomed home.

Then the present came rushing back, violent and bright and brutal. The Austin hit one of the boulders set along the edge of the road to warn travellers of the drop, striking it head on and with such force that the bonnet buckled. A spasm of pain shot up through me as my head snapped back, then jerked forward and hit the dashboard.

After that, nothing.

The Watcher in the Hills

Whispering. I could hear whispering, voices slipping between the mountains.

'*I am the last, the last, the . . .*'

Heard over the howling of the wind, sometimes far away, sometimes closer, so close I imagined I could feel breath upon my cheek.

'*The others have slipped away into darkness.*'

'Here,' I tried to say, but no sound came.

Then the sound of sobbing, a desperate scratching of rock upon rock, and a terrible weeping. *Piano, pianissimo, moriendo*, like the final strains of a country bell ringing out for evensong.

'Over here,' I murmured. 'Please. Help me.'

I can't be sure how long I was in this state, neither conscious nor yet quite unconscious. The sensation was like drifting underwater at the lido, swimming slowly, slowly up through the deep green water, closer and closer to the surface and the light. Sight, touch, sound. The tips of my fingers, the whiteness behind my eyes, my toes within my boots.

Then I was choking, coughing. Not drowning, waking. I was coming round. I could feel the pump and hiss of my heart beneath my ribs, rattling like a snare drum. I swallowed hard. When I put my hand up to brush the snow from my cheek, I saw that the tips of my gloves were red. And when I looked down, the snow and glass and blood were mixed together in my lap, glittering and yet dull at the same time.

I let my shoulders fall back against the seat. Even that slight movement caused the car to tilt and I knew I had to get out. It was balanced for the time being, but how long it would remain so was anyone's guess. Later, I learned that a shock absorber had snapped and the jagged metal had caught on the rocks beneath the snow.

I had a sense of the minutes counting down to some zero point. I looked at the clock on my dashboard. Last time I'd noticed, it had been coming up for two. Now the glass was shattered and the hands hung uselessly down at half-past six.

My head was throbbing. I steadied myself, then

leaned forward and released the catch on the door. The gusting wind immediately surged through the gap and sent the door slamming back against the wing, making the car rock. Cautiously, I swung out one leg, then the other, vaguely aware of being relieved that I was able to do so. I propelled myself into a standing position, sending the remains of the windscreen showering from my lap, then staggered away from the car. The wind boxed my ears so hard that I struggled to keep my balance, but I managed finally to get the door shut.

Hunching my shoulders against the bitter cold, I ran my hand along the coachwork, trying to assess the level of damage. I'd bought the Austin earlier in the year with the modest legacy left to me after the death duties had been paid on Father's estate. Its value was as much sentimental as financial. It was the last link between him and me.

The good news was that I was not seriously injured. And that the car had not gone over. The bad news that there was no possibility of getting it going again without assistance. Debris lay all around. Shards of glass crunched beneath the soles of my boots. The bonnet had buckled and the radiator had collapsed in on itself, like a broken ribcage. One of the front lamps had been snapped clean off and the other hung crooked, bashed up and attached to the body only by the thinnest of wires.

I knelt down in the snow. Metal and bits of pipe hung beneath the chassis. The torque tube had become detached and the running board stuck out at an angle, like a torn fingernail.

The cold was unlike anything I had ever experienced. It was no longer snowing, but there was a swirling fog, growing thicker by the minute, that wrapped itself around me, insinuating itself into my nose, my mouth, my throat. It muffled all sound and distorted the landscape, giving the countryside a sinister character. Misshapen trees and rocks transformed themselves into mythical beasts.

I pulled my cap as low as I could on my head. Even so, the tips of my ears were raw. My tweeds below the hem of my overcoat were already damp and heavy against my calves. Fresh blood trickled down my cheek. I pulled out a handkerchief and held it to the cut, a starburst of red on the pale blue cotton. It didn't hurt, but I knew from George that wounds rarely hurt straight away. Shock was Nature's anaesthetic, he'd told me. Pain came later.

There was nothing I could do but leave the car

and go for help. I couldn't even risk trying to get things from my suitcase for fear of sending the car right over the edge.

I looked round to get my bearings. Where was I? Closer to Tarascon than Vicdessos? Visibility was down to a few feet in both directions. The route I'd driven had all but vanished in the fog, and the road ahead was swallowed up by a curve in the mountain.

Then I remembered noticing a wooden signpost by the side of the road, lit up by the final flash of lightning. Since I had passed no houses, and had no hope that I would find any if I went higher into the mountains, it seemed a sensible idea to try to find it. Perhaps it indicated a footpath, and a path had to lead somewhere. Even if it did not, it would be more sheltered in the trees than on the bare mountainside.

I locked the driver's door, more out of habit than necessity, then, pushing the keys deep into my pocket, I turned up the collar of my coat, wrapped my scarf as tightly as I could around my neck, and headed back down the road.

I walked and walked, like Good King Wenceslas in the snow. The world had turned to white. Everything was stripped of colour, an absence of light and shade, not a bare patch of land in sight. The fog hovered motionless now in the branches of the trees, but at least the wind was easing a little. After the noise of the storm, it was all very still. Quiet.

Eventually, I found the sign. I brushed away the snow from the horizontal board, but there was no information on it, just an arrow pointing downwards. It didn't look promising, but it seemed the only option was to follow it.

To wherever it goes . . .

Then I heard it again. The same light voice, shimmering, indistinct, carried through the chill air.

'*I am the last, the last . . .*'

'What the Devil . . . ?'

I spun round, searching for the source of the sound, but could see no one. I told myself that if snow and the mountains played tricks on the eyes, on one's perspective, then why not on one's sense of hearing, too? There was no one. And yet I knew I was being watched. The short hairs on the back of my neck stood on end.

It came again, over the whistling of the wind, the same indistinct whispering.

'*The others have slipped away into darkness.*'

I stared up at the blurred horizon in the direction of the sound. And this time, on the far side of the valley above the tree-line, I swear I saw someone, something, moving. An outline, against the flat sky. My heart lurched.

'Who are you?' I cried, as if I could be heard from such a distance. 'What do you want?'

But the figure, if it had even been there at all, had vanished. Confusion kept me rooted to the spot a moment longer. Was it an illusion brought on by shock? A delayed reaction to the accident? How else to account for it? In such solitude any man might find himself inventing evidence of other human existence in order not to be alone.

I lingered, for some reason unable to tear myself away, until the cold got the better of me. Then, with a final glance over my shoulder, I stepped onto the path and headed into the woods, leaving the voice behind me. Leaving her behind me.

Or so I thought.

The Path Through the Woods

The footpath was overgrown and steep, just wide enough for two people to walk side by side. But as I'd hoped, the canopy of evergreen leaves had protected it from the snow. I could just make out the frozen ruts left by the wheels of a narrow cart and the hooves of a horse, or perhaps an ox. My spirits lifted a little. At least someone had passed this way, not too long before.

Soon I found myself at a crossroads. The left-hand path looked the more travelled. The oak and box dripped with winter. Everything smelt sodden, the leaves on the path and the sharp needles of the fir trees. The right-hand path was similar, box and silver birch, but it was much steeper. Rather than running in a zigzag, it plunged straight down the mountain-side.

I looked down at my boots. Fitwells were advertised as being equal to any weather conditions, though I hardly thought the manufacturers had mountaineering in mind. But they were holding up, though the cold seeped up through the soles, and my toes, even with two pairs of thick woollen socks, were frozen. My fingers, too. The bottoms of my trousers clung to my legs. The sooner I got out of the cold, the better.

So I took the right-hand path, assuming it to be more direct. It had an abandoned air to it, a feeling of neglect and stillness. There were no footprints, no wheel troughs, no sign the mulch on the ground had been disturbed. Even the air seemed colder.

The path was so precipitous that I was forced to brace my knees and steady myself on overhanging branches so as not to lose my footing.

The extravagant roots of ancient trees criss-crossed the path. Stones, uneven earth and fallen, fossilised branches, slippery with frost, jutted out from the dense thicket on either side. The atmosphere grew more claustrophobic. I felt trapped, as though the forest was closing in upon me. There was something grotesque about the landscape. Everything was both familiar and yet somehow distorted.

I could feel my nerves starting to get the better

of me. Even the animals seemed to have abandoned this strange and silent place. No birds sang, no rabbits or foxes moved in the scrub. I lengthened my stride, walking faster, faster, down the hillside. Several times I dislodged a stone and heard it tumble into the dimness below. Increasingly, I imagined peculiar shapes, outlines, behind every tree, eyes in the dark forest watching me pass. An unwelcome and persistent voice in my ear started to ask if it was more than just the storm that kept the people away.

In the deepest thickets of the forest, the light had all but disappeared. Mist was slinking through the trees, slipping in and out of the trunks and hollows like an animal hunting its prey. There was an absolute and impenetrable stillness.

Then I heard the snap of a twig underfoot. I stopped dead in my tracks, straining to hear. Another sound, the crunch of leaves and stone. Something was moving through the undergrowth. My heart skipped a beat. I knew there were wild boar in the Pyrenees, but were there also bears or wolves?

I looked for something to defend myself, before pulling myself up short. As if I could take on any kind of beast and hope to come off the better. My only resort, should I have the misfortune to encounter a wild animal, would be to stay absolutely still and hope it didn't pick up my scent. If it did, then there'd be nothing for it but to run.

Another sharp crack of a branch, closer this time. Galvanised into action, I cast around to see if at least there was a tree I might climb, but could see none with branches low enough to the ground. Then, to my intense relief, I heard voices. A moment later, two indistinct figures emerged from the mist on the path below. Men, two men, both carrying guns. One of them had a brace of woodcock dangling over his shoulder, their blind black eyes staring like beads of glass.

'Thank God,' I sighed.

Not a bear or a wolf. Half wondering if it might have been their voices I'd heard earlier, though it seemed unlikely from the look of them, I called out a greeting. The last thing I wanted was to be mistaken for the very animals I'd feared were tracking me, and end up with a bullet in me.

'*Salut! Quel temps!*'

They might be poachers and worry I would report them to the authorities, so I held up my hands as they drew nearer, to show I was no threat.

'*Messieurs, bonjour à vous.*'

They nodded but did not speak. Only a strip of skin was visible around their eyes, between the rim of the fur hats and their scarves pulled up over their mouths and noses, but I could see they were suspicious. I could hardly blame them. I must have looked a sight.

'*Je suis perdu. Ma voiture est crevée. Là-haut.*'

I gestured vaguely behind me in the direction of the road and attempted to explain what had happened – the snowstorm, the crash. I finished by asking if there was somewhere nearby where I might find help. At first, neither man reacted. I waited. At last, the taller of the two turned and pointed down the path. It led to a village called Nulle, he said in a gruff voice thick with tobacco and smoke. The hunter held up both hands and flexed all ten fingers once, then again. I frowned, then realised he was trying to tell me it was a twenty-minute walk. At least, I assumed that's what he meant.

'*Vingt minutes?*'

He nodded, then put his finger to his lips. I smiled to show I understood. They were without permits, then.

'*Oui, oui. Je comprends. Secret, oui?*'

He nodded again and we parted company. They

continued up the path and I carried on down, feeling unaccountably rather cheered by the exchange. Before long, the slope levelled out and I found myself on a patch of flat ground that looked out over a valley to the mountains on the far side. The sky seemed brighter and there was no snow on the fields, just the faintest hint of frost on the furrowed earth. Then, beyond a row of bare trees, signs of life. A twist of smoke wreathing up into the air.

'Thank God,' I sighed again.

The village sat in a dip between the hills, surrounded on all sides by the mountains. Red-tiled roofs, grey stone chimneys and, in the centre, higher than all the other buildings, the spire of a church. I picked up the pace, keeping the steeple and bell as the fixed point in my sights. I was already imagining the comforting clatter spilling out from the cafés and bars, the rattling of crockery in the kitchens, the sound of human voices.

There was a bridge in the furthest corner of the meadow. I made for it and crossed quickly, surprised to see the stream was flowing. I would have thought the rills and brooks would be frozen from November to March at such altitudes. But the water was racing along, lapping against the bottom of the bridge and splashing up over the banks. I heard the thin tolling of the church bell, the mournful single note carried on the air.

One, two, three . . .

I was surprised that so little time had passed since I'd abandoned the car on the road. But I knew as well as the next man how our experiences mould themselves to fill the time allocated to them. It was easy to believe that shock and the foul weather had muddled my sense of time.

I listened until the bell died away, then stepped off the bridge and carried on across the meadow. Here, autumn appeared not to have entirely relinquished its hold on the land. Instead of the barren grey and white of the mountain passes, there were the reds and copper of fallen leaves. In the hedgerows I could see tiny splashes of colour, flowers of blue and pink and yellow, like confetti scattered in a churchyard after a wedding. I even picked out broom, and autumn poppies growing tall. Bright red, like splashes of blood against the white frosted tips of the green grass.

The meadow gave way to an earthen track, wide enough for a cart or a car to pass along. Its surface was slippery and once or twice I felt my boots all but slide from under me, though I stayed upright.

Finally, I came to a small wooden sign telling me I had arrived in Nulle. I hesitated, looking back over my shoulder at the soaring mountains with their cloak of trees, sheer against the winter sky. I was suddenly reluctant to leave them behind me. The thought of having to find lodgings, explain my predicament once more, the effort required to organise the rescue of my car, all of it seemed beyond me.

And there was something more. I have gone over this moment many times in the past five years and, still, I have no idea why instinctively I knew there was some kind of cloud, some sadness, hanging over the village. That something was not quite right, was misaligned, like a picture askew on a wall.

I shook my head. I was in no position to find fault. I was cold and tired. There would be time enough, once I found lodgings, to consider the events of the day. I pushed my hands deeper into my pockets and walked into the village.

The Village of Nulle

The storm had clearly passed over the valley, leaving it untouched, for there was no snow at all on the road or the roof tiles.

I walked slowly, trying to get the measure of the place. I passed a handful of low buildings which looked like stores or animal pens. Drips of water had frozen along the guttering in rows of icy daggers pointing sharply down at the hard ground below. Notwithstanding the fearsome cold, the village seemed oddly deserted. No boys with delivery carts selling milk and butter. No post office vans. In the houses, I saw an occasional shadow move in and out of the slivers of light that slipped out between partially open shutters, but no one out and about. Once I thought I heard footsteps behind me, but when I turned, the street was empty. Other sounds were rare – a dog barking and a strange, repetitive noise, like the rattling of wood against the cobbles – and vanished into the mist as quickly as they had come. After a while, I began to wonder if I had imagined them.

I walked further. Then my ears picked out what sounded like the bleating of sheep, though I knew that was unlikely in December. I'd been told of the twice-yearly *fête de la transhumance*, the festival in September to mark the departure of the men and flocks to winter pastures in Spain, then again in May, to celebrate their safe return. Throughout the upper river valleys of the Pyrenees, this was a fixture on the annual calendar, a time-honoured tradition of which they were proud. More than once I'd heard the Spanish slopes described as the '*côté soleil*' and the French side of the mountains as the '*côté ombre*'. Sunshine and shadows.

The houses grew more substantial and the condition of the road improved, though still I saw no one. On the end walls of the buildings were tattered advertising boards promoting soap or own-brand cigarettes or aperitifs, and ugly telephone wires stretched between the buildings. Everything in Nulle seemed drab and half-hearted. The colours on the posters were bleached and dull, the paper peeling at the corners. Rust flaked from the metal fixings on the wall that held the wires in place. But there was something about the stillness of the afternoon light, the ambience of being down-at-heel, that I liked, like a photograph of a once-fashionable destination that had now grown old and tired. I felt oddly at home in this forgotten village, with its air of having been left behind.

By now I had arrived at the heart of the village, the place de l'Église. I tipped my cap back on my head – the snow had seeped through to the headband and was making my forehead itch in any case – and took stock. In the centre of the square was a stone well, a pail dangling from a black wrought-iron rail that arched across it. From where I stood, I could see a *bistro-café*, a *pharmacie* and a *tabac*. All of them were shut. The awning above the *café* was shabby and hung loosely against the wall, as if even it had long since given up hope. The church filled one side of the square, flanked by a line of plane trees, their silver bark mottled like the skin on an old man's hand. Even they seemed disconsolate, abandoned. The street lamps were already alight. I say lamps, but in fact they were old-fashioned *flambeaux*, real torches of fire and pitch burning in the open air. The dart-ing flames cast criss-cross patterns down through the bare branches of the trees to the cobbled stones beneath.

My eye was drawn by a narrow building, larger than the rest, with a wooden sign hanging on the wall. A boarding house or hotel, perhaps? I walked quickly across the square towards it. Three wide stone steps led up to a low wooden door, beside which hung a brass bell. Its thick rope twisted in the currents of cold air, round and round. A hand-painted board above the door announced the name of the proprie-tors: M & MME GALY.

I hesitated, conscious of the fact that I looked pretty disreputable. The cut on my cheek was no longer bleeding, but I had specks of dried blood on my collar, my clothes were wet and I had no luggage to recommend me. I looked wretched. I straightened my scarf, pushed my stained handkerchief and gloves down into the pockets of my overcoat and adjusted my cap.

I tugged on the bell and heard it ring deep inside the house. At first, nothing happened. Then I heard footsteps inside, coming closer, and the sound of a bolt being drawn back.

A snaggle-toothed old man, in a flat-collared shirt, a waistcoat and heavy brown country trousers peered out. White hair framed a lined, weather-beaten face.

'*Oui?*'

I asked if there might be a room for the night. Monsieur Galy, or so I assumed, looked me up and down, but did not speak. Assuming my French was at fault, I pointed down at my wet clothes, the wound on my cheek, and began to explain about the accident on the mountain road.

'*Une chambre – pour ce soir seulement.*' One night only.

Without taking his eyes from my face, he shouted over his shoulder into the silence of the corridor behind him.

'*Madame Galy, viens ici!*'

From the gloom of the passageway, a stout middle-aged woman appeared, her wooden *sabots* clacking on the tiled floor. Her greying hair was parted in the centre and pulled off her forehead into a tight plait. It gave her a somewhat severe look, an impression reinforced by the fact that, save for her white apron, she was dressed entirely in black from head to toe. Even her thick woollen stockings, visible beneath the hem of her calf-length skirt, were black. But when

I looked at her face, I saw she had an honest, open expression and kind brown eyes. When I smiled, she smiled warmly back.

Galy waved his hand to indicate I should explain once more. Again, I began to recite the litany of mishaps that had led me to Nulle. I did not mention the hunters.

To my relief, Madame Galy seemed to understand. After a brief and rattling conversation with her husband in a heavy dialect too thick for me to follow, she said of course they could provide a room for the night. She would also, she added, arrange for someone to accompany me into the mountains tomorrow to retrieve the automobile.

'There is no one who could help now?' I asked.

She gave an apologetic shrug and gestured over my shoulder. 'It is too late.'

I turned and was astonished to see that, in the few minutes we'd been talking, dusk had stolen the remains of the day. I was on the point of remarking upon it, when Madame Galy continued to explain that, in any case, this particular day in December was the most important annual celebration of the year, *la fête de Saint-Etienne*, observed since the fourteenth century. I did not catch every word she said, but understood she was apologising for the fact that everyone was caught up in preparations for the evening's festivities.

'*Il n'y a personne pour vous aider, monsieur.*'

I smiled. 'In which case, tomorrow it is.'

And I was reassured. No doubt, here was the reason for the strange, hushed silence of the village, for all the shops being closed, for the queer burning *flambeaux* in the square.

Beckoning for me to follow, Madame Galy clattered down the corridor. Monsieur Galy shut the front door and bolted it behind us. When I glanced back over my shoulder, he was still standing there frowning, his arms hanging loose by his sides. He seemed unhappy about the appearance of an unexpected guest, but I wasn't going to let it bother me. I was here. Here I would stay.

There was a round switch for an electric light on the wall, but no bulbs in the ceiling fittings. Instead, the passage was lit by oil lamps, their small flames magnified by curved glass shades.

'You have no power?'

'The supply is not reliable, especially in winter. It comes and goes.'

'But there is hot water?' I asked. Now I was out of

the cold, I was able to admit how utterly done in I was. My thighs and calves ached from my trek down into the village and I was chilled right through. More than anything, I wanted a long, warm bath.

'Of course. We have an oil heater for that.'

We continued down the long corridor. I glanced into rooms where the doors stood open. All were empty. There were no sounds of conversation, of servants going about their duties.

'Do you have many other guests?'

'Not at present.'

I waited for her to elaborate, but she did not, and despite my curiosity, I did not press the point.

Madame Galy stopped in front of a high wooden desk at the foot of the stairs. I caught the smell of beeswax polish, a sharp reminder of the back stairs leading up to my childhood attic nursery that were so dangerous for boys in stockinged feet.

'*S'il vous plaît.*'

She pushed an ancient register towards me. Leather binding, heavy cream paper with narrow blue feint lines. I glanced at the names above mine and saw that the last entries were in September. Had there been no one since then? I signed my name all the same. Formalities accomplished, Madame Galy chose a large, old-fashioned brass key from a row of six hooks on the wall, then took a lighted candle from the counter.

'*Par ici,*' she said.

Chez les Galy

I followed Madame Galy up the tiled staircase, twice catching the toes of my boots on the timber nose of the treads.

On the first landing, she held up the candle to illuminate a second flight of steps, and we stumbled on in Indian file, until she stopped in front of a panelled door and unlocked it.

'I will have a fire made up.'

The room was bitterly cold, though it was clean and serviceable, with the same lingering smell of polish and dust as downstairs.

While Madame Galy lit the oil lamps from the candle, I looked around. A small writing table and cane-seated chair stood adjacent to the door. Straight ahead, two tall windows, floor to ceiling, filled one side of the room. Against the left-hand wall was an old-fashioned bed on wooden pallets. Brocade curtains, of the kind my grandmother used to have, sagged round the bed on brass rings. I tried the mattress with my hand. It was uneven and hard, with a hint of damp from lack of use, but it would do me well enough.

On the opposite side of the room was a heavy chest of drawers, a lace runner draped across the top, on which stood a large white china bowl and wash jug. Above it hung a gilt-framed mirror, its bevelled surface scratched around the sides.

The cut on my cheek had started to sting. I put my fingers up to the wound and felt the blood had congealed and hardened. I asked if I might have some ointment.

'The smash,' I said, feeling the need to explain. 'Bumped my head on the dashboard.'

'I will bring something up for it.'

'It's good of you. There is one more thing. I need to send a telegram to my friends in Ax-les-Thermes.'

'We have no telegraph office in Nulle, monsieur.'

'Somewhere closer by, then? Is there perhaps someone with a telephone?'

Madame Galy shook her head. 'In Tarascon, of course, but such conveniences have not yet come to the valley.' She pointed at the table. 'If you care to write a letter, I will send a boy to Ax in the morning.'

'Ax is closer?'

'A little, yes.'

It still seemed an awfully long way to go, but if it was the only option, then so be it.

'Thank you,' I said, then shivered. 'I don't want to be a nuisance, but I was obliged to abandon my suitcase. In the car. So, if you had something I could borrow for the night, I'd be grateful.'

Madame Galy nodded. 'I will find something for you to wear while your clothes are drying.' She paused. 'Should you wish to join us, monsieur, the celebration for *la fête de Saint-Etienne* will begin at ten o'clock. You would be most welcome.'

'That's kind of you, madame, but I would hate to intrude.' Given the day I'd had, I thought it unlikely I'd even still be awake at ten o'clock.

'You would not be intruding, not at all.'

Madame Galy was smiling at me now and, despite my tiredness and aching bones, I found myself warming to her. Her enthusiasm was engaging.

'It is the one night the village comes together,' she continued, as if she were reciting from a brochure issued by the local tourist office. 'It is the custom to wear traditional dress – weavers, carders, soldiers, the good men even – whatever a person chooses.'

'The good men?' *Les bons hommes*. I'd heard the phrase before, but I couldn't recall where or when.

'It is the night we remember old friends and new. Those that are amongst us still, those that have gone.' Her voice trembled a little. 'Those who were lost.'

'I see.'

This was a change from most of the other places I had visited, where I'd found a resolute determination to forget the recent past and move on. That Nulle honoured its history and clung to its traditions, even if for only one night a year, appealed to me.

'You say *la fête* begins at ten o'clock?'

'Ten o'clock, monsieur, in the Ostal. It is not easy to find, since many of the streets are unnamed in the oldest *quartier* and several alleyways are now dead ends. But I could provide you with a map, should you decide to join us.'

I had been looking forward to having something to eat and then the chance to turn in early. I was not at my best in strange company, too often shy or tongue-tied. But, against the odds, I found myself attracted by the idea of attending.

'You are quite sure I would not be imposing?'

She shook her head. 'You would be most welcome.' She paused. 'Besides, I regret there will be no hot food here this evening. We are all commandeered to help at the Ostal from six o'clock.'

I laughed. 'That settles it. I shall certainly accept the invitation. And your offer of a map, too.'

She smoothed her hands on her apron and beamed at me, evidently pleased things were settled, and at that moment reminded me of no one so much as the smiling, maternal face of Mrs Bun the Baker's wife in my old card deck of Happy Families.

'And will Monsieur Galy be attending?'

The smile slipped from her face. 'The night air does not agree with him,' she said quietly. 'The cold gets into his bones.'

She placed the key on the table and, reverting to her brisk, matter-of-fact voice, added, 'The bathroom is at the end of the corridor on the right-hand side. I will draw a bath for you, then see to a fire and your clothes.'

'Thank you.'

'If there is nothing more you need?'

'Nothing, thank you.'

She nodded. '*Alors, à ce soir.*'

Once she had gone, I removed my boots and damp socks, which were starting to itch, then emptied the contents of my pockets on top of the chest of drawers. My keys, my cigarette case and matches, my pocket book. Then I sat down at the desk. There were several sheets of notepaper, as well as a rather antiquated pen with a scratchy nib. The inkwell, surprisingly, was full. The paper was not headed, so I cast my eyes around for some official notice that might reveal the actual address of the boarding house. There was a sign pinned to the back of the door about what guests should or should not do in case of an emergency or a fire, but nothing more. In the end, I simply put c/o M & MME GALY, LA PLACE DE L'ÉGLISE, NULLE, ARIÈGE, and left it at that. I had no doubt any reply would find me easily enough.

I scribbled a few lines to my friends, saying I'd be delighted to join them, if they'd still have me, and that, since I had no idea how long it would take to repair my motor car, I would be in touch again in a day or two to let them know when to expect me.

There was no blotting paper, so I waved the sheet about and blew on the ink until it was dry. There were no envelopes, either, so I folded the letter over on itself three times, printed the address of my friends' hotel in Ax-les-Thermes on the outside and left it on the table to take down later.

I stripped down to my undergarments. Despite my exhaustion, I was in good spirits. As I took the clean towel from the end of the bed and went in search of the bathroom, I realised I was whistling.

The Man in the Mirror

When I got back to my room after a long, hot soak in the bath, a fire was burning in the grate, releasing an aroma of pine resin into the room. The smell snapped at my heart strings, taking me back to Sussex winters when I was a boy, with George home from school for the holidays.

Madame Galy had brought a brass-handled oil lamp with a round wick burner and bulging glass chimney, and set it on the table. A tray with a glass and heavy-bottomed bottle had also appeared on the chest of drawers.

It was all very congenial, snug.

My trousers were draped over a wooden clothes horse set at an angle in front of the fire. I rubbed the heavy tweed between my fingers. Still damp, but well on the way to being wearable. My slipover was on a lower rung, the arms dangling down, and my socks were drying on the hearth, the toes, where the wool was thickest, pointing towards the flames. Of my overcoat, cap and boots there was no sign, nor of my shirt. It occurred to me that Madame Galy was soaking it to try to shift the blood on the collar.

She had been as good as her word and found clothes for me to borrow. Rather, a costume. I picked up the tunic of rough cotton from the bed, and smiled. The sleeves only reached the elbow, there was no collar and there were ties at the neck in place of buttons. It was much like the sort of thing I'd once worn for a particularly dreadful school production of *A Midsummer Night's Dream*.

I'd been to a couple of costume parties in London in the days after the War had ended and before my nerves got the better of me. I had enjoyed them. I liked the anonymity of disguise, for a few hours pretending to be a man of action from history or the pages of a novel. A Shackleton or a Quatermain.

I was still stiff from the accident, so eased the tunic carefully over my shoulders, then stepped back to take a look at myself in the mirror. Dressed as a peasant with my hair sticking up as nature intended, I was hardly Mr Rider Haggard's hero. But I was pleased enough.

I looked closer and felt something shift inside me, for, despite the cracks and breaks on the bevelled surface, staring back at me from the mirror was a reflection I had not thought to see again. Myself. Or, rather, the person I might have been had not grief marked me. The lines of loss, of illness, were still there. I was too pale and thin, that was undeniable, and my green eyes were perhaps a little too bright. But the features were familiar. My old self was making its way to the surface. Freddie Watson, younger son of George and Anne Watson, Crossways Lodge, Lavant, Sussex.

I looked a while longer, happy in my own company, until my bare feet started to ache with cold. I hurried to finish dressing. Madame Galy had left no trousers to match the tunic, so I presumed she intended me to wear my own. The turn-ups were still a little damp, but they'd do. I slipped them on, buttoned the fly, then thumped down on the bumpy mattress to investigate the footwear that had been left in place of my boots.

I examined them in the light cast by the oil lamp. They, too, had a theatrical look. Soft leather boots with no heels or fastenings. They set my memories racing once more. A family outing one Christmas when Mother took George and me to see *Peter Pan* at the Lyric Theatre. The afternoon stuck in my mind because it was rare for her to accompany us. We ate jellies in the interval and Mother, her peaches-and-cream complexion pretty in the dimmed light of the theatre, scrutinised the audience and the latest fashions. For some months afterwards, George and I adopted Pan's catchphrase of how to die would be an 'awfully big adventure' and thought ourselves amusing.

I looked down at the boots in my hand. They were precisely the kind of things the boy playing Peter had worn. I could hear George in my ear, joshing me for even contemplating putting on such footwear.

'A step too far, old chap, a step too far,' he'd have said. I could hear the dry humour, the inflection of his voice. His words poking me in the ribs.

'A step too far, not bad,' I said. 'Not bad at all.'

I felt the smile slip. The truth of it was that these words belonged to me, not George. I so wanted to hear him talking to me in that low, wry way of his, the distinctive fall at the end of every sentence, that charming, cracked tone partway between boredom and brilliance. But however hard I tried to keep my end of the bargain, the conversation was always one-sided.

Was it in that little room in Nulle that the realisation struck me? How I'd fallen into the habit of ascribing every witty, clever aphorism to George? How I'd stepped out of my own life and into the wings, yielding centre-stage to him? Or was it something I already knew but had not wanted to acknowledge?

But I do know that, as I let the leather costume boots drop from my hand to the floor, I was aware of something slipping away from me. Of something being lost.

'An awfully big adventure,' I muttered.

I sat for a moment longer, then strode over to the chest of drawers and poured myself two fingers from the bottle. It was a thick, red liqueur, and I swallowed it down in one gulp. A little sweet for my taste, it nonetheless hit the back of my throat with a kick. Heat flooded my chest. I poured another double measure. Again, I downed it in one. The alcohol knocked the edge off things. I was reluctant now to leave the warm cocoon of the room. Taking a cigarette from my case, I tapped the tobacco tight and paced the room as I smoked, this time enjoying the texture of the cold wood beneath my bare feet. Thinking about the day, thinking about things.

I flicked the end of the cigarette into the fire, then

crouched down to see how my socks were doing. The movement set the room spinning.

'Food,' I muttered. 'I need food.'

They were dry, though stiff as a board, and I rubbed and stretched at the wool before pulling them on. The boots were tight, and looked rather peculiar matched with tweed trousers, but not otherwise too bad a fit.

I was ready. I gathered up my bits and pieces from the chest of drawers, and took the hand-drawn map Madame Galy had left as promised. Then, with a last look around the room, I picked up the letter and went out into the cold corridor.

There was no one downstairs, though the oil lamps were burning. I put the letter in plain view on the high reception counter then, leaning across it, I called into the gloom of the back rooms beyond.

'*Monsieur Galy? Je m'en vais.*'

There was no answer. As I drew back, I saw I had left the imprint of my hands on the polished wood. The problem was I had not thought to ask how I should get back in to the boarding house later. Would I need a latchkey? Should I ring the bell or would the door be unlocked?

'Monsieur Galy, I'm off now,' I called again.

There was still no response. I hesitated, then slipped round behind the desk and replaced the room key on its hook so he would see that I had gone.

An antique tall case-clock with a mahogany surround stood in the alcove beneath the sweep of the stairs. I looked up at the mottled, ivory-coloured face, at the slim Roman numerals and delicate black hands. There was a whirring of the mechanism inside the case, then a high-pitched carillon started to chime.

I knew I'd taken my time but, even so, I was surprised that it was ten o'clock already. In the sanatorium, sedated by my physicians, whole days had passed in the blinking of an eye. On other occasions, blunted by the medicines they force-fed me morning and night, the world seemed to limp to a standstill. Even so, had seven whole hours really gone by since first I'd arrived at the boarding house? No wonder I was hungry.

My overcoat was hanging on a hook on the wall beside the front entrance. I shrugged myself into it, put on my cap, then I pulled open the heavy door and stepped out into the night.

La Fête de Saint-Etienne

The place de l'Église was deserted. Already there was a hard frost and the ground beneath my feet glistened white. It was very still and very pretty, like glitter on a Christmas card. The *flambeaux* were burning fiercely.

Holding Madame Galy's map in my hand, I headed diagonally across the square towards the church and the maze of tiny streets that made up the oldest *quartier* of the village where she had indicated the Ostal would be found.

I walked past the plane trees, then down a narrow and nondescript alleyway by the side of the church. The cold pinched at my cheeks and my hands, so I walked quickly. In the few moments it had taken me to cross the square, a low mountain mist had descended, shrouding everything in a shifting, diaphanous whiteness. It curled around the buildings and the street corners.

I walked a little faster. The impasse de l'Église led to a labyrinth of winding, cobbled back streets, each apparently identical and giving no indication as to where they might lead. I knew I was heading in the right direction, but though Madame Galy had marked the correct passageways to take, it was not clear which was which. And while people had left their lights burning in houses in the square, here in the old *quartier* it was very dark indeed. The houses were all shuttered and the windows hidden.

I lit a match and peered at the map, trying to orientate myself in relation to the place de l'Église and the church, before setting off again. I found myself at a crossroads, which was not marked on Madame Galy's map. I wasn't usually such a dolt, but the lack of street signs and the slinking mist weren't making it any easier.

Then I heard voices, fragments of conversation, laughter, splinters of sound carried through the narrow alleyways on the night air. I folded the map and put it in my pocket, deciding to trust my instincts instead. I picked up the pace, following one path, then another, until I saw light ahead and abruptly emerged from the warren of little streets.

Straight ahead of me was a large rectangular building, much like the old wool market in Tarascon. Night had stripped it of colour, but it resembled all the other municipal town halls I'd seen in the southern towns through which I had passed. The ubiquitous pale limestone of the Pyrenees and the sloping roof made it appear both modest and imposing at one and the same time.

A colonnade ran along the front with three high arches. Shallow steps stretched the width of the building. The dust of the passing years seemed to have accumulated in the nooks and crevices of the stone. Substantial wooden double doors in the centre stood open, spilling out a rectangle of welcoming yellow light into the December evening.

Anticipation fluttering in the pit of my stomach, I climbed the steps and found myself in some kind of entrance hall. It was barely warmer inside than out. Ahead of me was a huge door, some ten feet high or more and decorated with carvings of fruit and heraldic symbols, subtle shapes and images on the dark wood.

I took off my coat, marvelling at the seriousness with which the citizens of Nulle approached their annual celebration. For rather than the usual collection of evening jackets and coats and stoles, there were rows of cloaks in plain blues and reds and greens and browns hanging on the black iron hooks. My overcoat looked oddly modern and fussy in such company.

I took a few deep breaths to steady my nerves, then tugged sharply down to straighten my tunic, and walked through the door with as much confidence as I could muster.

The heat hit me. A warm fug of people and roaring fires and conviviality. Noise, too, deafening after the stillness of the old *quartier*, a cacophony of laughter and chatter, the clattering of dishes and waiters moving to and fro. I stood quite entranced on the threshold, mesmerised by the scene laid out before me. The air was thick with smoke from the open fire burning at the far end of the room, a thousand candles scattered light and shadow from metal sconces on the walls, ever shifting, ever dancing. I scanned the hall, hoping to catch sight of Madame Galy, but there were too many people to pick out just one in the crush.

As my eyes adjusted, I got the measure of my surroundings. The hall was twice as long as it was wide with a high, vaulted ceiling. The stone walls were bare, no paintings or photographs or ornamentation of any kind. A long refectory-style table stood across the top of the room and two more lined the walls, each covered with heavy white cloths and surrounded by benches. Only at the top table were there chairs.

Then, floating above the polyphony, a descant to the obligato of the crowd, a single thread of music. The distinctive open chords and plain melody of a *vielle*. Moments later, a clear, treble voice began.

> *Lo vièlh Ivèrn ambe sa samba ranca*
> *Ara es tornat dins los nòstres camins*
> *Le nèu retrais una flassada blanca*
> *E'l Cerç bronzís dins las brancas dels pins.*

I did not understand the words but I caught their spirit and somehow knew he sang of the mountains, of winter, of the snow and the pine trees. An old ballad in an antique language. All the time he was singing, the music held me in its spell, filling my head with images and emotions that had been long absent. My eyes pricked with tears.

Once, years ago, I'd tried to explain to George what I felt when I listened to a choir sing, when I heard the reverberation of the plainsong in the upper echelons of the cathedral or the stalls of our little country church in Lavant, but he didn't understand. Music never moved him and although he would sit and listen to me play the piano for hours, I knew his thoughts were elsewhere. He sat there for me, not for himself.

'*Monsieur, soyez le bienvenu.*'

The voice startled me back to the present. I turned to see a man with a shock of copper hair and an open, thoughtful face smiling at me.

'Hello, thank you.' I held out my hand. 'Frederick Watson. Madame Galy said I should look in. I'm lodging there for a day or two.'

'Guillaume Marty.'

Since he did not offer his hand in return, though his expression was welcoming, I let mine drop.

'Wonderful turnout,' I said.

'All who can be are here, yes.' He nodded. 'Please. Follow me. I shall find you a place to sit.'

Marty was dressed as a priest or a monk in some kind of religious get-up, but the long green robe did not seem to inhibit him and he moved quickly through the crowds. He wore sandals on his feet and a leather belt around his waist, from which hung a scroll or rolled parchment. He looked utterly the part. Again, I marvelled at the lengths to which the inhabitants of this tiny village had gone to make sure the evening went off well.

As we made our way through the hall, Marty was stopped many times. Two smiling sisters, Raymonde and Blanche Maury, dressed in royal-blue robes with red stitching around the neck and cuffs; Sénher Bernard and his elderly wife; the widow Na Azéma, as she was introduced, her hair covered by a grey veil pinned beneath the chin; Na and Sénher Authier, the latter a large gentleman whose high colour and broad arms suggested eating and drinking were his vocations in life. After several more such introductions, I realised that Na and Sénher were a local form of madame and monsieur. I noticed a woman who looked very like my landlady, and was on the point of waving when she turned and I realised it was not her.

'Is Madame Galy here?'

'I do not believe I have seen her.'

The contrast between the feelings of sadness that had come over me when I'd first entered the village and this convivial gathering could not have been more marked. Here, in the Ostal, the sense of community and camaraderie was tangible. Everyone was smiling and nodding as we passed, offering friendship.

Guillaume Marty stopped and indicated I should

sit at one of the few remaining spaces on a bench. I threaded myself in, all clumsy elbows and knees. When I turned to thank him for seeing me right, he had already disappeared again, swallowed up by the crowd. I leaned back and glanced up and down the room, but could see the green robe nowhere.

'Queer that he didn't say goodbye,' I murmured. 'Pity.'

I turned my attention to my immediate dinner companions. To my right was a man of about my age, with rough brown hair the texture of straw, thick black brows and dirty fingernails. He sat hunched over the table. His dark tunic, belted at the waist, was stained with grease and red wine and meat, a map of the meals he had eaten. His eyes flickered with curiosity, quickly masked. I smiled and he nodded a half-greeting, but did not speak.

I turned to my left.

If I were a wordsmith I could, perhaps, begin to do justice to my first impressions of the girl who sat beside me. As it is, a plain description will have to do. She was the sort of creature that Burne-Jones or Waterhouse might have painted, exquisite and perfect, and I, untouched by beauty for so long, felt my heart take flight. Her dark hair tumbled in loose curls around a porcelain face, unspoiled by powder or rouge. A wide, pretty mouth, also left as nature intended, made even more appealing by laughter lines at the corners.

She must have felt the intensity of my gaze, clearly, for she turned and stared back at me. Clever, grey eyes rimmed by long lashes. I gawped like an idiot.

'Frederick Watson,' I said, finally remembering my manners. 'Freddie. My friends call me Freddie.'

'I am Fabrissa.'

That was it, that was all she said. But it was enough. Already, her voice was familiar to me, beloved.

'What a charming name,' I said. My brain seemed disconnected from the rest of me. 'Forgive me, I'm . . .'

She smiled. 'It is difficult in unfamiliar company.'

'Quite,' I said quickly. 'One doesn't know what to expect.'

'No.'

She fell silent and, thankfully, so did I. I took a mouthful of wine to steady my nerves. It was a harsh rosé, with something of the bite of dry sherry, and it made me cough. She affected not to notice.

I was grateful for the activity around us. It gave me the chance to observe Fabrissa without being too obvious, sending sly little glances her way. Looking, then turning away. Gradually, I took in every detail of her appearance. A long blue dress, fitted at the shoulders and tapered at the waist. Sleeves, wide at the cuff and decorated there, and at the neck, with a repeated pattern stitched of white, interlocking squares. It matched the pattern on her embroidered belt – a girdle, I suppose – which was blue and red against a white background. The overall impression was plain, yet elegant, nothing trying too hard to make a statement. No fuss. Dazzling in its simplicity.

Slowly, we managed to find a way of talking to one another, Fabrissa and I. With the help of the sour, rich wine, my pulse slowed to its usual rhythm. But I was aware of every inch of her, as if she were giving off some kind of electric charge. Her white skin and blue dress and her hair the colour of jet . . . I felt awkward in comparison, and took refuge in innocuous questions, managing, against the odds, to keep my voice steady and calm.

Servants were circulating with tureens. When the lids were lifted, billows of aromatic hot cabbage and bacon soup were released, steaming leeks and herbs, which they ladled into dust-coloured bowls set at each place.

There seemed to be no sense of one course being

distinct from another. Flat grey platters appeared, heaped with broad beans in oil, mashed turnip, whole chickens, mutton and salted pork. On the opposite side of the room, a waiter carried high on his shoulders a wooden board bearing six trout, their silver scales glistening.

Fabrissa explained each new dish for me, local specialities, recipes I'd never encountered before. One was a peculiar *compote* of what she told me were medlars, an ugly fruit that had to be harvested and then ripened off the tree. It had the texture, the stickiness of honey. Another common winter dessert, she explained, was made from the flowerbuds of cardoons. Blanched and then wrapped in cloth, they were buried in the ground before being dug up and mixed with honey to make a smooth paste.

Other than food, I can remember little of what we talked about in that early part of the evening. Everything is hazy, filtered through the warm fug of wine and conversation. Inconsequential, but such agreeable conversation to me. I cannot even remember if she spoke to me in French, or I to her in English, or *moitié-moitié*, a duet in two languages. But, even five years later, I can still taste the tang of the salt pork on my tongue, still savour the rough, woody texture of the broad beans, slippery in oil, still feel the gritty texture of the bread, like crumbled cake, between my fingers.

And still I hear the song in my mind, though I never caught sight of the troubadour. His voice floated through the hall, up into the rafters, into every stone corner and dusty cobweb. I remember marvelling that he could sing for so long, with a tone so even and unbroken, and I believe I said so. I think I might even have tried to tell her of the musical aspirations I'd once had before the War intervened and Father decided it was not a suitable career for his son. But I drew back from such confidences. I wished neither to burden her, nor to reveal myself as a man disappointed in life. Instead, I asked her to tell me the story of the ballad, and when she had, in return I explained the accompaniment, how one note worked upon the other to provide its own harmonies.

So time passed and yet did not move at all. And, for me, enchanted as I was, the world had shrunk to her slim white hands, the promise of her tumbling black hair, her grey eyes and her clear, sweet voice.

'Are you an honest man?' she said.

'I beg your pardon?'

I started, taken by surprise both by the question

and the grave tone in which she asked it. It was so different from the lightness of our conversations before that I hardly knew what to make of it.

But I answered. Of course I answered.

'I would say so,' I said. 'Yes.'

Fabrissa then tilted her head to one side in that distinctive way of hers and looked at me.

'And a man who can tell true from false?'

I paused as I considered how to answer. Ten years of voices in my head, of memories that were more real, more vivid, than the world outside my window. Ten years of living with George at my side. All this would suggest I was very far adrift from reality, that I was incapable of distinguishing true from false. But at that moment, sitting with Fabrissa in the warm companionship of the Ostal, the answer was obvious.

'Yes. When it matters, then, yes. I am.'

She smiled, a broad and hopeful smile. And I, poor slave, felt a thousand emotions explode inside my head. I was lost. Bewilderingly, heart and soul, lost. Still she stared at me, as if seeking the answer to some question she had yet to ask.

'Yes,' she said finally. 'I can see it.'

A whistle slipped silently from between my lips. I felt as though I had passed some kind of test. A modern Gawain setting out from the Round Table, the conditions of his quest met. I was aware of her gaze upon me, weighing up the man I was. I could see she was considering and reflecting, I could see the movement in her eyes. But on the outside she was still, so very still. I tried to be the same, though nerves were sloshing in my stomach like bilge water in a scuppered rowing boat.

The moment stretched between us. The shapes and sounds and smells of the room, all the guests in it, faded away. Then Fabrissa shifted position on the bench and the enchantment was broken.

'Tell me about him,' she said.

The ground fell from under me, like a trapdoor beneath the hangman's noose. A sudden, sharp drop, then the jerk of the rope.

How did she know? I had said nothing. Hinted at nothing. I did not want to talk about George, not even to Fabrissa. Especially not to Fabrissa. I did not want her to see me as the wretch I believed myself to be, but rather the man I had been for the past hours in her company.

'What do you mean?' I said, more sharply than I intended.

She smiled. 'Tell me about George.'

Still I pretended not to understand.

'Freddie?' she said quietly. Her hand slid across the rough white cloth, a little closer to mine. Her finger-nails were the colour of pearl.

I took a sharp intake of breath. 'I can't.'

'Why not?'

'I . . .'

How to explain? I stumbled for an excuse.

'It's all been said.'

'Maybe only the wrong things have been said.'

Her hand was so close to mine now that we were almost touching. I noticed how the gold ring she wore on her right thumb was too big for her. It rested on the knuckle, as though surprised to find itself there.

'Talking doesn't help.'

The space between her skin and mine crackled. I dared not move. Dared not let the tips of my fingers stray towards hers.

'Talking did not help,' I repeated, the words dry in my throat. I glanced at her. She was still smiling, not with pity, but with compassion, curiosity. I felt something crack inside me.

'And could it be you talked only because others required it of you? Maybe? But it is different here. Things are different. Try.'

'I did try,' I snapped back, appalled at how immediately the sense of being unfairly judged returned. Mother had accused me of not wanting to get well, Father too. I could not bear it if Fabrissa thought the same. 'No one believed me, but I did try.'

Whether by design or accident, her hand brushed against mine as she withdrew it from the table and placed it in her lap. So intense, so profound was the sensation, I felt as if I had been burnt.

'I—'

'Try again, Freddie,' she said.

And in those three quiet words, three simple words, somehow there was a promise of an entire life to be lived if I could only take the chance.

I can still recall the sense of possibility that came over me then, a kind of lightness. Every sinew, every muscle, every vein in my body seemed suddenly to vibrate, to be alive. If I could find the courage to speak, she would listen. Fabrissa would listen.

I took a deep breath and then slowly, steadily, exhaled. Finally, I began to talk.

Stories of Remembrance and Loss

'I remember everything about that day,' I said. 'Every tiny detail. The smell and the texture of it, every second before and after the knock at the door.

'I was in the nursery toasting bread. Cross-legged on the floor, a slab of butter ready on an old green china plate. It was September, but with the promise of autumn to come. The purple leaves on the copper beech were turning and there was condensation on the inside of the windows in the early morning. The fire had been lit for the first time since the previous winter and there was the bitter, musty smell of singed dust in the chimney.

'On the wall above my bed was pinned a hand-drawn map of Europe printed by the *Manchester Guardian*. It was covered with red crosses, my attempt to mark each place the Royal Sussex Regiment had been – at least, where I imagined my brother's division might be. Where George might . . .' I stopped, the stab of memory too sharp.

Fabrissa waited. She seemed to have no need to hurry me or require me to turn fragments into a single, clear narrative. Her patience rubbed off on me, and when I found it in me to continue, the sequence of events was clearer in my mind and the words I needed came, if not easily, then at least less hesitantly than before.

'I didn't hear the knock at the door. But I remember being aware of our maid's footsteps on the flagstones in the hall. Florence always did shuffle and fail to pick up her feet. I was aware of the door being opened and mumbled words, too faint for me to make out.

'Even then, I think I knew. There was something in the quality of the silence which shouted out that this caller was unwelcome. I stopped what I was doing and listened, listened to the silence. Then my mother's clear, shrill voice in the hall. At the door. Yes, yes, I am Mrs Watson. And, moments later, a single word, so much the worst for being spoken so softly: "No."

'The fork dropped from my hands. I can see it now, falling slowly down, metal clattering on the hearthstone, toe, heel, toe, like a tap dancer, before coming to rest. The bread, so perfectly burnt on one side and raw white on the other. I ran. Sending the door flying back against the wall, I ran down the nursery stairs in my stockinged feet. On the same old dangerous turn, I slipped and lost my footing, cracked my shin. Blood started to seep through my sock and, absurdly, I remember thinking how I would be scolded for being so clumsy.

'Down to the first landing, along the passageway where the carpet began. From the hall below, a sound that tore through me like a butcher's knife. Not screaming exactly, more a howling, a wailing, the same word repeated over and over, "No, nooooo", becoming one, single note.'

I stopped again, the memories too painful. I glanced at Fabrissa, seeking her reassurance and that she really did want to hear this.

She nodded. 'Please, go on.'

I held her glance, then fixed my eyes back to the same spot on the table.

'It was the fifteenth of September, did I say that? Almost two years to the day since George had enlisted. I had seen him once or twice, of course. He had been injured and sent home twice. A problem with his ears after a bombardment, not too bad. A bullet in his thigh the second time, again not life-threatening.'

I shrugged, a casual gesture concealing the anger I felt with the doctors, with my father, for letting him go back to the Front at all, though I knew it was what he had wanted. It was a thin line between hero-ism and arrogance, and George had always walked it. We were the Watson boys. Nothing could harm us. He had believed in the myth of his own invincibility, whereas I? I had always felt the world was a danger-ous place, waiting to spring its traps.

'Both times, they patched him up and sent him back. But we hadn't had a letter in a while, not since May. He was due home for a couple of days' leave, so I tried not to be worried. Also, that summer I'd been ill with a serious bout of influenza, so I'd not been able to follow the progress of George's battalion in the newspapers so closely.'

I stared at my hands, at the lines on them. They were no longer the hands of a child pushing pins into a map on the wall.

'The worst of it was that no one talked to me. Not then. Not later. No one told me anything. When I got to the hall and ran to my mother, she lashed out at me, as if she could not bear to have me in her sight. Not hard, but I stumbled back against the hall table, sending a bowl of late pink roses in a crystal vase crashing to the ground. Water and glass and torn petals all over the rug. It was left to Florence to take me to the kitchen and dab iodine on my shin. She was crying. Her cap was all awry. They were all weeping, Florence and Maisie and Mrs Taylor, our cook. They loved him, too.

'Mother shut herself away in the drawing room until Father came home. I could hear them talking behind the closed door. I pressed my ear against the polished wood, praying that they would know I was there and allow me in. Comfort me. But they didn't. And although I knew that there had been a telegram and that everything was spoiled, nobody told me what it said. What, precisely, had happened to George. They simply forgot about me.

'I was fifteen, but I stationed myself halfway up the stairs, as I'd done when I was a boy, watching the front door, my head resting against the banister, my arm wrapped around the spindles for comfort. I sat there for hours, watching the setting sun shine through the stained glass and throw beams of red and blue onto the flagstone floor.'

'Willing George to come?'

I shrugged. 'I don't know.'

Softly, gently, she reached out and covered my hand with hers. Her skin was cold, her touch insubstantial, so light, as if she were barely there. But I was overwhelmed by the understanding implicit in her gesture. Grateful for her care.

'It was only some time later I learned the telegram said George was missing in action. I never understood why the news had taken so long to reach us. It had happened weeks before, weeks and weeks. The thirtieth of June. The Battle of the Boar's Head, a place called the Ferme du Bois outside Richebourg l'Avoué. The day before the Battle of the Somme began. Missing in action, the telegram said. Not dead. So I was confused. I thought – hoped – that there was some doubt. Perhaps the Germans had taken him prisoner. Perhaps he was in hospital having lost his memory. I was furious with my parents for believing the worst so easily. For not holding firm to the idea he could be alive.

'Later, they sent his things home through Cox's. Damp and worn and rigid with mud, the smell of the charnel house and barbed wire and gas. His cap was missing. The garter badge and Roussillon plume he was so proud of were gone. But there was a waist-coat, stiff with blood, and his braces.' I swallowed hard. 'It was only when I overheard Florence talking to the ironmonger's boy at the back gate that I realised George's body had been so devastated there was nothing left to identify. Almost the entire Thirteenth Battalion, the Southdowners, was wiped out. They knew he was dead all right, mown down with his men. It's just they couldn't distinguish one body from the next.'

'And so you became ill?'

I shook my head. 'Not then, later. The breakdown, collapse, petit mal, neurasthenia, nerves, whatever you want to call it. It didn't come out straight away. Not until I reached the age George had been when he died. My twenty-first birthday, in fact.'

'You did not speak of your grief?'

I shrugged. 'Who would have listened? Within a mile of our house, twenty, thirty families were in the same boat. The Battle of the Boar's Head is known as "The Day Sussex Died". Hundreds of local men, boys like George, went to war and never came back. There's a plaque on the wall of the memorial hall in my home village listing some thirty men, of all ranks, who fell that day. The same thing in all the villages around us. And there was always another battle coming up behind, worse and bloodier and less inexplicable. I suppose I thought I had no right to make a fuss. That I was old enough to cope. Certainly, my parents thought so.'

'They were not aware how much you suffered?'

'I'm not sure it would have made any difference. You see, it was George they loved. It wasn't that they were deliberately unkind, only that mourning George drained the life from them. That I might be missing him too did not cross their minds. And, for my part, in my muddled, old-fashioned way, I saw they had a better claim to grief than did I, so I said nothing.'

'Your parents are gone?'

I nodded. 'Mother passed away last winter. Father earlier this year.'

'And do you miss them?'

I was on the point of muttering the usual platitudes, but I stopped. What was the purpose in lying? Good manners, tradition, fear of painting a poor picture of myself? The truth was I felt relief, not loss. Now they both were dead there was no longer any need to pretend. They had been unable to love me. But that was their fault, not mine.

'Sometimes,' I said eventually. 'Every now and then, something will happen and I will think of them. I have a few happy recollections. But for the most part, it is easier without them.'

I looked again at Fabrissa. She did not seem disapproving or shocked. Her skin was almost transparent now in the flickering candlelight, as though the effort of listening was draining the colour from her.

'I like to think that I would have been able to accept his death if only I had believed it was true. Grieve, yes, but move on. If only I had accepted he was dead. But I couldn't bring myself to believe it. Not for years. The idea he would never again come whistling through the door, or sit in the leather armchair in the music room blowing smoke rings at the ceiling while I banged away at some Beethoven sonata on the piano, was too absurd.

'It was this, I think, the not knowing, that preyed on my mind. Not knowing what had happened to him, how he had died, when he had died. I became obsessed with piecing together those last minutes of George's life. I read every report in the newspapers I'd missed when I'd been ill. Studied everything about the battle at Richebourg l'Avoué that I could lay my hands on – the terrain, the weather reports, the ratio of their men to ours. I sought out those few men of the Southdowners who'd survived the engagement and wrote to ask if they had seen him.' I shrugged again. 'Made everyone's life a misery.'

'The dead leave their shadows, an echo of the space within which once they lived. They haunt us, never fading or growing older as we do. The loss we grieve is not just their futures but our own.'

She was speaking so quietly now that I strained to hear her over the noise of the room.

'But that was not what made you ill,' she continued. 'Not the fact of his death, but what followed.'

I took another gulp of wine and felt the room stagger. I'd had more than enough to drink, but knew I needed to blunt my memory if I was to finish the story.

'Whatever I did made no difference,' I said in a level voice. 'I tried to make up for the fact that George was dead. Be twice the son. But it was George they wanted back, not an imitation of him. They wanted the son who played rugby and cricket and went to war, not a sickly, indoors boy, a boy who cared more for music and books than riding or hunting or skating on the river in winter when the Lavant froze over.'

I was twisting a loose thread of cotton from the

tunic round and round my index finger, so tight it was cutting off the blood supply. The soft skin at the tip turned white, then purple. The sensation was comforting.

'Ironically, in the light of my parents' antipathy to my penchant for reading, it was a book that did for me in the end. George's final gift to me, sent from the Front in December nineteen fifteen, wrapped in brown paper and string.'

I paused. 'Most of all, it was the burden of guilt. In six years, I never did crawl out from under its shadow. In the end, I no longer had the will to fight it. It just seemed easier to give in.'

'Why should you feel guilt?'

I sighed. 'Everything. I don't know. It made no sense, but it's how I felt. Guilty for being the wrong son, that I'd been too young to fight, that I was alive when George was not.' I swallowed hard. 'Most of all, guilt that I was learning to live without him. It seemed an act of betrayal.'

'A betrayal of whom?'

'George.' I waved a hazy hand, feeling the wine singing in my veins. 'Of us. Not rational, I know.'

'To survive when others do not takes a particular sort of courage,' she said softly.

'Yes,' I sighed, relieved she understood. 'And here's the thing. It seems idiotic now, but in the days and weeks after the telegram arrived, I tried to bargain. I'd say to myself – to a God I no longer believed in – that if George is not dead, then I will not read this book or I will not play this *étude*, or do this thing or that. Stupid wagers I can't even remember now.' I pulled the thread of cotton tighter, jerking savagely at it until it snapped. The pressure gone, I felt the blood rush back to my finger. 'Missing in action. Missing presumed dead. We had no body to bury. No funeral. No headstone to mark his passing.'

Fabrissa nodded. 'It did not feel as if it were over.'

I shook my head. 'I only understood this when they dedicated St George's Chapel in Chichester Cathedral as a memorial to those men of the Royal Sussex Regiment who had lost their lives. It was the eleventh of November nineteen twenty-one, the anniversary of the Armistice. That's when it hit home, his complete and utter absence. That nagging, unanswered question about where precisely he had fallen. How, precisely, he had died. His name was on a list for all to see, but what did that mean? There was a memorial, too, a pale stone cross in Eastgate Square, and another list in the new memorial hall erected on our village green. But George was not there, either.'

'But he understood. And so you withdrew into another place, to be with him.'

A wave of gratitude washed over me that this beautiful stranger, this girl, should grasp things so clearly, when those who should have known me best had not.

'I held out for six years. But it came in the end, my breakdown, collapse, whatever one calls it. December nineteen twenty-two. I was taken to a private hospital, a sanatorium for men with nerve problems, neurasthenia and other consequences of having survived the trenches. The medical staff was kind and efficient.' I glanced at Fabrissa. 'But I did not want to get better if it meant losing what little I had left of my brother.'

There. I had said it. I exhaled. My shoulders sagged, worn out by the act of confession. All the emotions, all the regrets and questions I'd allowed to decay inside me for so long, lay scattered about, like discarded gifts. Then, the faintest of smiles came to my lips. I did feel less burdened. Wrung out, certainly, but for the first time since that September day in 1916, my tattered heart was at peace.

Silence fell between us. And in that silence, all the

words said and not said seemed to sing. And within it, the whole world was contained, accounted for.

'But now, it is time to let him go. It is time to walk out of the shadows. You know this.'

My eyes snapped open. There was something in the echo and tone of her voice that sent a different kind of memory scuttling across the surface of my mind. A connection between Fabrissa's clear voice speaking to me in the Ostal and the whispering on the road to Vicdessos.

'Freddie.' It was as if she breathed rather than spoke the word. 'You know this. You would not be here else.'

That voice. Her voice. How could it be? Could the mountain air have played such a trick, distorting and changing my perspective?

'It was you,' I said at last in disbelief, yet knowing I was right. 'It was you I heard.'

Under Attack

She turned her face away.

'Fabrissa?' I said urgently. 'Was it you in the mountains, earlier, before the snow started? Was it? Did you see me? Fabrissa, please.'

Still she did not answer. I would have pressed her further, except I was suddenly aware the atmosphere in the Ostal had changed. The air was charged with anticipation, with tension.

I tore my eyes away from Fabrissa for a moment. While we'd been talking, everything else had receded. Now, like the lights coming up in the auditorium at the end of a concert, the world came back into focus. The white tablecloths, no longer pristine but covered instead with empty dishes, splashes of spilt wine and crumbs of bread, chicken bones and mutton grease.

The noise level had dropped. Like the low growl

of an Easter tide sucking back from the seashore, the rumble of voices was constant, but muted. Everyone seemed to be speaking in hushed voices. Hooded and watchful eyes, no laughter now. For the first time since sitting down at the table, I felt uncomfortable.

I turned back to Fabrissa, but she had withdrawn into herself. And when I said her name she started violently, as if she had forgotten I was there.

'Fabrissa,' I repeated gently. 'What is it? What's happening?'

She looked at me, then, with an expression of such regret, such longing, that my breath caught in my chest. I forgot myself, instinct making me reach out to her and put my arm around her narrow shoulders. Beneath the heavy cotton of her robe, she was so thin, so fragile. Skin and bone, hardly there at all. But as I held her, I felt my heart sing, expand and soar free. Then she moved, as if my touch pained her, and although she did not ask me to, I withdrew my hand.

Then I felt something. A piece of rough material, different in texture from the rest of her gown. Gently, I lifted her hair and saw there was a crude yellow fabric cross, about the size of a man's hand, stitched to the back of her blue dress.

'What is this?' I asked.

Fabrissa shook her head, as if it were too complicated to explain. Now I noticed what I had previously missed; namely, that several of the other guests had the same yellow crosses pinned to their tunics or to the backs of their robes.

'Fabrissa, what do they signify?'

She did not answer, but I could see she was uneasy. The air felt heavy now, weighted. Everyone was waiting for something to happen, I could feel it. A shiver ran down my spine. I reached for my cup, forgetting it was empty.

'Damn it.'

It was probably a good thing. Everything was a little blurry round the edges. I was half-cut already.

Then I heard, quite distinctly, the stomp of horses' hooves outside in the street, and the rattle of harness. I frowned. Who would be out at this time of night and in such temperatures?

'Nothing here can harm you,' she said. 'No one.'

After her long silence, her voice was startlingly loud, and I swung round in alarm.

'Harm me? What do you mean?'

But her eyes had clouded over again. I was baffled. Didn't know what to make of it, any of it.

I turned to my right. The man was still hunched

over the remains of his meal, but he had stopped eating. Up and down the table, across the room, it was the same story. Anxious faces. Frightened faces. Those to whom Guillaume Marty had introduced me earlier: the timeworn Maury sisters and Sénher and Na Bernard, holding hands; widow Azéma, her old milky eyes looking into the middle distance. Again, I searched for Madame Galy, knowing the sight of her would be somehow reassuring, but still could not see her.

The hall seemed colder and I felt the same sense of desolation when I'd first arrived in Nulle, except now the sadness was tinged with fear.

At the far end of the room, an altercation broke out. Voices raised, the sound of a bench being overturned. At first, I assumed it was some kind of drunken brawl. It was late and the wine had flowed freely all night.

Fabrissa turned towards the entrance. I did the same, at the precise moment the heavy wooden door was flung open. Two men strode into the hall.

'What the Devil . . .'

Their faces were concealed beneath square iron helmets and the candlelight glinted on their unsheathed swords, sending flashes of gold dancing around them like sparks from a blacksmith's anvil.

For a moment, nobody spoke. Briefly I wondered if

this was part of the evening's entertainment. Some absurd historical re-enactment of the original, long-gone *fête de Saint-Etienne* taken too seriously. Like the costumes or the traditional foods or the troubadour and his *vielle*.

Then a woman screamed and I knew it was not. Panic took hold. My uncouth dining companion scrambled to his feet, shoving me with his elbow. I fell against Fabrissa and felt her heavy hair briefly touch my skin, a subtle scent of lavender and apple.

'Freddie,' she whispered.

A small group of men was attempting to drive the intruders from the hall. Some brandished hunting daggers, drawn from their sheaths on their belts. Others grabbed at whatever makeshift weapon came easily to hand: pieces of wood, irons from the fire, even the heavy skewer on which the meat had been served.

The blades jabbed and sliced the air, though never connected. It was an unequal fight for, although the soldiers had the advantage of heavier weaponry, they were overwhelmingly outnumbered. The crowd was shouting and pushing forward now in a mass of arms and legs. The cry went up to barricade the door. The mood was ugly, likely to escalate. I did not want Fabrissa to be caught up in it.

And despite the exhaustions of the day, despite the fact that it must have been well past midnight, I felt suddenly alive. Purposeful. Adrenalin coursed through me. This time I wouldn't funk it.

I reached for Fabrissa. 'We must leave.'

'Are you sure?'

Her tone was grave, as if my rather obvious suggestion held some significance beyond simple common sense. I took her hand. An intense heat shot through my veins, carried the singing in my blood to the base of my spine. I seemed to grow taller. I felt capable of anything.

'Come on. Let's get you away from here.'

Did I manage to keep the smile from my face? Looking back, I'm sure I did not because, finally, my hour had come. All my life I'd been second best. Never the right man for the job. Not invincible.

Not George.

That night it was different. Fabrissa had put her trust in me. Had chosen me. It was a gift I'd never thought to receive. And even now, more than five years after the event, and in the light of everything that subsequently happened, the ecstasy of that moment will never leave me.

'Is there another way out?'

She pointed to the far corner of the hall.

The soldiers had been driven back, but now there was fighting everywhere, between those marked out by a yellow cross and those not. I felt I was observing the scene from above, disconnected and yet at the heart of things. Holding on to Fabrissa tightly, I launched forward into the mass of bodies, swimming against the tide. We ran, she and I, clumsily hand in hand.

'Through there?' I said, raising my voice to be heard. I could see a small door set in the wall, partially hidden behind a pyramid of wooden chairs and a heavy wooden chest with a metal clasp and bands.

She nodded. 'It leads to a tunnel that runs beneath the Ostal.'

With a strength I didn't know I possessed, I hauled the chest aside and tossed the chairs out of the way as if they were made of pasteboard.

Was I scared? I should have been, certainly, but I don't believe I was. Instead, what lingers in my memory is my single-minded determination to get Fabrissa to safety. I unhooked the latch and pushed at the door with the flat of my hands until there was a gap wide enough for us to slip through. We ducked under the low lintel and down into the darkness we went.

The steps were shallow, worn away at the centre, and I held her hand even tighter to prevent her from slipping. In the hall above, I could hear women screaming and men shouting instructions and children crying. The sound of wood splintering and the clatter of metal on metal. Then the door thudded shut at our backs and we were plunged into silence.

I hurtled forward, but was forced to slow down. I couldn't get the dimensions of the tunnel fixed in my mind. The air was dry at least, not damp, with a smell that reminded me of cathedrals and catacombs, of all those hidden places lying forgotten across the long and dusty years. A cobweb draped itself across my face, my mouth and eyes. I spat the filigree threads away, though the sensation lingered.

'Shall I go ahead of you?' Her voice was soft in the dark. 'I have been this way before.'

I squeezed her hand to let her know I was fine with things as they were, and felt her return the pressure. I smiled.

'Where does the tunnel come out?'

'On the hillside to the west of the village. It is not far.'

The Yellow Cross

We stumbled along in the dark. After our initial descent, the tunnel quickly flattened out for a while, before beginning slowly to climb again. My breath came in ragged bursts and sweat gathered on my temples and cheeks, making my cut sting.

I concentrated on keeping my footing. I could see nothing at all. The roof of the tunnel seemed sometimes to skim my head, and the walls were close enough to touch, but I had no sense of where we were. Fabrissa, though, seemed unchanged. She appeared to be neither tired nor breathless in our claustrophobic surroundings.

So we pressed on, on through the subterranean world, until the atmosphere began to alter. The path grew steeper still, and I felt a whisper of fresh air on my face.

The ground suddenly veered precipitously up-wards. The perspective ahead of us slipped from black to grey. Pinpricks of moonlight gleamed around what looked like a door blocking the end of the tunnel.

I sighed with relief.

'There is a brass ring,' said Fabrissa. 'It opens in-wards.'

I ran my fingers over the surface of the wood, like a blind man, until I found it. The handle was cold and stiff. I grasped it with both hands and pulled. It didn't shift. I braced my feet apart, and tried again. This time, I felt the door straining at the hinges, though it still didn't budge.

'Could it be barred from the outside?'

'I do not think so. It is probably because this par-ticular escape route has not been used for a very long time.'

There wasn't time to wonder what she meant. I just kept at it, pulling steadily, then following it up with a series of sharp jerks, until finally there was a dull crack and the wood around the hinges splintered.

'Nearly,' I said, pushing my fingers in the gap be-tween the door and the frame.

Fabrissa put her hands below mine and together

we tugged and wrenched until, suddenly, we were outside in the chill night air. Behind us, the door hung loose on its hinges, reminding me of the entrance to an old copper mine George and I had discovered one wet August holiday in Cornwall. He, of course, had wanted to go in, but I'd been too scared.

Different times, different places.

I turned to Fabrissa, standing so still in the flat, white moonlight.

'We did it,' I panted, trying to catch my breath.

'Yes,' she said softly. 'Yes, we did.'

We were standing out on a bare patch of ground about halfway up the hillside, to the east of the village. The opposite side of the valley, I realised, from the direction in which I had approached Nulle the previous afternoon. I felt light-headed, intoxicated by the night air, by what we had achieved, by her company.

Then I felt a stab of guilt I could not ignore.

'I must go back. I have to do something. Help. People could be seriously hurt.'

She sighed. 'It is over now.'

'We can't be certain of that.'

'All is quiet,' she said. 'Listen. Look.' She pointed down at the village. 'All is calm.'

I followed the line of her finger and picked out the church spire, the patchwork of houses and buildings and alleyways that made up Nulle. The Ostal itself, white in the moonlight, was directly below us. Nothing was stirring. No one was about. No lights were burning. I could hear nothing but the enduring silence of the mountains.

'It was all part of the *fête*?' I said. 'The soldiers, the fighting?'

But much as I wanted to be persuaded there was no need for me to intervene, it had seemed too brutal to be mere play-acting.

'Come,' she said quietly. 'There is little time left.'

'Where are we going?'

'To a place we may sit and talk a while longer.'

Fabrissa set off down the hillside without another word, giving me no choice but to follow. She walked fast, her long blue dress swishing about her legs. Beneath the swing and sway of her hair, I caught glimpses of the yellow cross. Without thinking about what I was intending to do, I hurried to catch up with her.

'Wait,' I said. With a sharp tug, I pulled the tattered piece of fabric from her back. 'There. That's more like it.'

She smiled. 'Why did you do that?'

'I don't rightly know. It looked wrong. Like it shouldn't be there.' I hesitated. 'Do you mind?'

I felt her grey eyes sweep across my face, as if committing every part of it to memory. She shook her head.

'No. It was brave.'

'Brave?'

'Honourable.'

While I was still pondering her choice of words, Fabrissa had set off again. I pushed the cross of fabric into my pocket and followed.

'So, what do the crosses signify? I saw several of the other guests wearing them, too.'

She did not answer and she did not slow down. The night air seemed to shift as she passed, and there was something about the translucent moonshine that gave me the impression she was made of air or water, rather than blood and bone. I did not press her further. I did not want to disturb the delicate balance between us, and that seemed more important than any questions I might want answered.

The path wound down through the frosted grass. I glanced over my shoulder and saw the mouth of the tunnel diminishing behind us. We were close to the village now, but rather than continuing down into Nulle, Fabrissa led me to a small dewpond halfway down the hillside and indicated we should rest. I sat down on the mossy trunk of a fallen tree, grateful for the chance to take the weight off my feet. The soft-soled boots had begun to pinch.

The sky was beginning to turn from black to inky blue. When I looked back up at the track, I could just make out the silver imprint of my footprints on the grass in the early-morning dew. Dawn was not far away.

I thought for a moment of the strangeness of dew in December, then how queer it was that I was not cold, despite having abandoned my coat and hat in the Ostal. I felt curiously weightless, as though, having spent the night in Fabrissa's company, I had taken on some of her qualities of delicacy and lightness.

I looked down into the still surface of the water. My cheeks were hollow with lack of sleep and my eyes, rimmed with exhaustion, stared back at me in the uncertain daybreak. Fabrissa's reflection was less clear. I turned, scared that she might have slipped away. But she was still there.

'I feared you had—'

'Not yet,' she said, reading my mind.

'We don't have to go back.'

'There is still a little time left.' She smiled. 'I should like to tell you something of myself, should you have the heart to listen.'

My heart leapt. 'Anything you want to tell me, I would be honoured to hear.'

I hadn't smoked all night, I suppose because nobody else had. Hadn't even thought about it. But now I fished in my pocket and pulled out my cigarette case and matches.

'Do you mind?' I said, taking one out and tapping it on the silver lid.

Fabrissa leaned towards me. 'What are they?'

'Gauloise,' I replied. 'I'm a Dunhill man in the normal run of things, but they're impossible to get down here.'

I offered the case to her. She shook her head, but seemed transfixed by what I was doing. She watched intently as I put the cigarette in my mouth, then cupped it with my hand, struck the match and held it against the tip. Her eyes grew wide as a wisp of smoke wreathed up into the dawn air and she reached out, as if to wind it around her fingers like thread.

'It is beautiful.'

'Beautiful?' I laughed, charmed. 'That's one way of

putting it, I suppose.' I snapped my case shut, returning it and the matches to my pocket. 'You're remarkable. I can honestly say I've never met anyone like you before.'

'I am no different from anyone else,' she said.

I smiled, thinking both how wrong she was and how delightful she did not realise it.

Fabrissa's Story

We sat in silence for a while. I smoked. She fixed her eyes on the dark horizon, as though counting the stars. Were there actually stars? I can't remember.

Then I heard her catch her breath and knew Fabrissa had been arranging her story in her mind, as I had done. I crushed the remains of my cigarette beneath the sole of my boot and turned to listen. I wanted to know everything about her, as much as she would tell me, anything. Tiny details. Irrelevant, beautiful details.

'I was born on an afternoon in spring,' she began. 'The world was coming back to life after a hard winter. The snow had melted and the streams were flowing again. Tiny mountain flowers of blue and pink and yellow filled the fields of the upper valley. My father used to say that on the day I was born, he heard the first cuckoo sing. A good omen, he said.

'Our neighbours came with a loaf they had baked, white flour, not coarse brown grain. Others also brought gifts: a brown woollen blanket for winter, furs, an earthenware cup, a wooden box containing spices. Most precious, salt wrapped up in a piece of cotton, dyed blue.

'It was May. Already, the shepherds and their flocks had returned from their winter pastures in Spain and the village was full of life and sound – the women chatting in the square, the wooden treadles of their looms clattering on the cobbled stones.'

She paused. I was happy to wait. I wanted to let her tell her story at her own pace, in her own way, as she had allowed me to do. Besides, the pleasure of listening to her voice was such that she could have recited a laundry list and still it would have rung like music in my ears.

'My birth was seen as a sign that things might be changing for the better,' she said. 'And my mother and father were well liked and respected in the village. They were loyal, honourable people. My father wrote letters on behalf of those who could not read or write. He explained the ways of the courts to those who needed representation or his help. Each fulfilled the role most suited to his character.'

'I see,' I said, though I did not.

'After years of violence and denunciation, it seemed our enemies had set their sights elsewhere and, for a while, we were at peace. There were, of course, the usual struggles, disagreements common to communities living in the shadow of war. But they were isolated incidents, not part of a systematic reprisal. And although we all knew someone who had been taken, most people were released with no more than the punishment of wearing the cross.'

Instinctively, my hand moved to my pocket. I took out the scrap of material and laid it across my knee.

'This was a way of marking people out?'

I looked down at the tattered piece of cloth, the yellow faded and sour. I had heard of the Germans inflicting penalties on civilians – *The Times* had written of it – but nothing like this.

'It was intended to humiliate, certainly,' she replied. 'But when so many were branded in the same way, it became a sign of good character.'

'A badge of honour.'

'Yes.'

Realising now it might be a symbol of her survival and that, therefore, she might wish to keep it, I held it out.

'I'm sorry, I shouldn't have taken it.'

She shook her head. I hesitated, then returned it to my pocket. It was hardly an orthodox love token, but it was all that I had.

'The raids became more frequent. Whole villages arrested, or so it was said – men, women, children. In Montaillou, little under a day's walk, everybody over the age of twelve was taken before the court in Pamiers. The interrogations went on for weeks. People talked of it in hushed whispers, behind hands and closed doors. Even so, we hoped our village was too small to matter to anyone but us.'

For the second time in so many days, my schoolmaster's dusty words came back into my mind.

'A green land soaked red with the blood of the faithful,' I murmured.

The effect of my words on Fabrissa was immediate. Her eyes lit up.

'You know something of our history?'

'Very little, I'm afraid. Only that this region is no stranger to conflict.'

'You will know, then, of the endless years spent fearing those we loved would be taken from us in the night. Never knowing whom to trust, that was the worst of it. Seduced by promises of safety and wealth, there were those who became spies. Who betrayed their own. I feared our enemies, but did not hate them.' She hesitated. 'But those who turned away from who they were and joined the fight against us, it was hard not to despise them.'

I nodded. In the early days of the War, I suppose it must have been during George's first leave home, I'd overheard him and Father talking through the study door, left ajar. I remember him explaining how he bore no hatred towards the ordinary German soldier, the men like him who fought for their country, fair and square. Father nodding, 'Yes, yes', and the air thick with cigarettes and whisky. But for those who would not fight, the Conchies, or those who spied for the other side, he had nothing but disgust. And as I listened in the hall, excluded from this man's world, I heard the admiration in Father's voice. And, God help me, I was jealous.

'I didn't realise the Germans were active in this part of France,' I said, as much to myself as to Fabrissa, trying to push away the unhappy memories. I knew the roll-call of battles – Loos, Arras, Boar's Head Hill, Passchendaele – each as notorious for the huge loss of life as for any supposed military success. But I couldn't recall any significant engagement below the Loire Valley.

'No,' she said. 'I was young, but already I knew that the war was not about faith, but rather territory and wealth and greed and power.'

'Yes,' I said, thinking of George's contempt for the politicians who sent good men to die.

The light was thickening, giving shape back to the world. I glanced at Fabrissa and saw how very pale her skin was, its patina almost blue in the dawn.

'Then, one day, it happened. The soldiers came for us.'

Exodus

My heart hit my boots.

'Look here, there's no need to . . . if it's too much.'

How I wanted to save her from the pain of remembering. How I wanted to put my arms around her and tell her everything was all right. But of course, it wasn't. How could it be?

Fabrissa gave a tiny shake of her head, but did not falter. And I understood that, having started, she needed to see things through.

'It was December,' she continued. 'A bright day, very cold, with a glancing white sun and blue skies. In the afternoon, the light lingered for just a little longer than usual on the mountains, golden light draped like a skein of silk across the snowed peaks of the Sabarthès, of the Roc de Sédour. Everywhere painted in gold and white. And although it went against what we believed, I remember thinking how hard it was not to believe that God's hand had created such a day.'

I looked at her then, touched by so simple a statement of faith. Already, the joy of that memory had gone. Her expression was serious once more.

'When night fell, everyone went to the Ostal for the *fête*.'

'The *fête de Saint-Etienne*?'

She nodded. 'There was a rumour that soldiers had been seen in Tarascon, but we assumed it was too distant to concern us. We suspected, too, that our enemies had lists of names, knowledge of possessions and old allegiances that they could only have been given by those who lived, hidden, amongst us.'

'Those who were not forced to wear the yellow cross?'

'It was not as simple as that,' she said, then paused. 'What we did not know, as we gathered for the feast, was that a troop of soldiers was already making its way up the valley. The rumours, this time, were true.

'My parents, my brother and I had spent the best part of the previous two days with my mother's family in Junac, on the other side of the valley. Our return journey had taken longer than expected, and the cold had taken its toll on my brother.'

'You have a brother?' I said under my breath, knowing, even as I said it, that it was idiotic for me to take pleasure in this similarity between us. 'An elder brother?'

'He was three years younger,' she said quietly.

'Was?'

She shook her head. I was furious with myself for having jumped in. Had I not yet learnt that Fabrissa would tell the story in her own way and in her own time?

'I'm sorry, I shouldn't have interrupted.'

'As we drew close to home, a boy came running out of the woods. He was in a state of shock, swallowing his words and talking too fast for us to hear what he was saying. My father managed to calm him and, with great patience, coax out of the terrified child that . . .'

She broke off, her eyes wide.

'That what?'

'That there had been massacres. That villages lower down the mountain had been put to the torch. Of old men, women, cut down where they stood. Children, too. Of the fields running with blood.'

I turned cold. 'Good God.'

'We had no way of knowing if the reports were

[145]

true, of course,' she continued. 'There had been many false alarms in the previous weeks. We could not be certain.'

I fished out another cigarette from my case and lit it.

'What did you do?'

'My brother's health was poor, so my father decided to take him and my mother home. He told me to go on ahead and that he would join me at the Ostal as soon as he could. Before we parted company, he made me promise to say nothing about the boy. True or false, his testimony would spread panic and alarm. Far better to wait until he could confer with the others and, together, decide what action to take.

'When I arrived at the Ostal, everyone was in good spirits. The whole village had come together to celebrate. My heart wept at the knowledge that in a matter of hours, this way of life might be lost.'

'That must have been very difficult.'

'So I sat, knowing what I knew and yet having to conceal it. And all the time, I was watching the door, waiting for my father. When he did come, he was immediately cloistered with Guillaume Marty, Sénher Bernard, Sénher Authier and the others.' Fabrissa hesitated. 'Later, I learned my father had questioned the boy further and satisfied himself that he was telling the truth without embellishment. He instructed my mother to pack what belongings we could carry between us and sent the boy round to rouse those who were at home, rather than in the Ostal. There were not many. Old Na Sanchez, who was bedridden, and Monsieur Galy.'

'Galy?'

'I knew none of this at the time, of course. I still prayed it might be a false alarm. My first indication it was not was the sound of horses' hooves and bridles outside, then two soldiers strode into the hall and the uproar started.'

I turned cold.

'The fighting escalated quickly. The soldiers were easily driven back and the doors barricaded shut. The spies in our midst had come armed, ready to support the attackers. But they, too, were swiftly overpowered.

'The very presence of the soldiers was proof that the main battalion was on its way. The tactic of sending scouts ahead was commonplace. Usually, the arrests were quick and undertaken without bloodshed. But this time, things were different.

The horrifying reports of the massacres in the valley suggested as much. My father and the others knew we had to flee the village before the main force arrived.

'Not everyone was prepared to go. Raymond and Blanche Maury said they were too old to be driven again from their homes and that they would rather die in their beds. But mostly people did as they were instructed and left the Ostal, by means of the underground tunnel. The *bons homes*, Guillaume Marty and Michel Authier, elected to stand firm and try to hold the soldiers off.'

My head was spinning with so much information. So much confusing, baffling detail.

'My mother had worked quickly. She and my brother, together with all those who had decided to leave, had packed what little they could carry – a loaf of bread, some beans, wine, blankets – and were waiting at the exit to the tunnel.

'The journey was hard for my brother. He was a sickly child, with little strength to see him through the long winters. I could see in his face how much pain he was suffering, although he never complained.' She stopped again. 'He never complained, not once.'

'What was his name?' I asked gently.

'Jean. His name was Jean.'

For a moment, we were silent, the threads of history flapping around us like ribbons in the wind.

'Where did you go? Was anywhere safe?'

'There are caves within these mountains, hidden from view.' She pointed across the valley, over the sleeping roofs of the village, to the woods through which I had made my approach into Nulle.

'The tiniest openings in the rock face lead to tunnels, ancient hiding places, a labyrinthine sequence of passageways and caverns.'

Thinking of the road signs I had seen yesterday for the caves of Niaux and Lombrives, I looked back in the direction we had descended, trying to work out how they had crossed from this side of the village to the other without being seen by the soldiers.

'And these caves were substantial enough to accommodate all of you?'

'There are whole cities underground, magnificent, soaring caverns.' Again, the same half-smile.

'Astonishing.'

'Yes. We travelled as far as we could by cart, until the ground became too steep. We unharnessed our mule, trusting she would find her way back home. Others did the same. We hoped, too, that the tracks left by the hooves of the animals and the wheels of the trap would serve as a false trail for the soldiers hunting us.

'We doubled back around the village, through the woods to the east, avoiding the open ground. Then we began the steep ascent up to the caves.'

'I still don't see how so many of you managed to evade the soldiers.'

'We knew the terrain, they did not, and we were lucky. That night there was no moon. Besides, the main contingent was further away than we had feared.' She paused. 'We covered the ground slowly, keeping always in the shadows and the protection of the trees. We carried no torches. No one spoke.

'There are two paths up through the forests on the far side of the village. One is very sheer, overhung by box and silver birch trees. The other path is longer, but it is less steep and also wide enough for two people to walk side by side.'

'I came that way, down from the road, through the woods towards Nulle from the east.'

'It was still night when we reached the halfway point where the two paths converge. My brother was struggling to carry on. He said nothing, but it was clear that he could not go much further. So rather than continue with the others, my father decided we should rest for a while then try to catch them up at first light. He had a memory of a harder but more direct path up to the caves that he had stumbled upon when he was a boy and not visited since. If his recollection was correct, he said, a sharp incline led to a plateau that should bring us out close to where the others were heading.

'We took leave of our friends, wishing them well and hoping to see them the following morning. We burrowed into the undergrowth and huddled together for warmth, wrapping ourselves in the blankets to wait out the night.

'Jean was quiet, though I could tell from the gulp and plash of the breath in his chest that he was weeping. I gave him wine and coaxed him to eat a little bread. I dared not sing to him to help him sleep, but I stroked his hair and held him tight, trying to keep his thin, shivering body warm. Little by little, his breathing became steadier and, at last, he slept. As did I.'

At the Break of Day

'I was woken by my father shaking me. It was a grey dawn. We could hear the soldiers shouting to one another down below, their coarse words carried on the thin morning air to where we lay hiding. They must have known we could not have gone far. We knew none of those who had stayed behind would betray our whereabouts, though I feared for their safety.'

'Were they . . . ?' I left the question hanging.

'We did not see them again,' she said simply.

There was no need to say more.

'Jean was weaker. The night air and the horror of the situation had further reduced his strength. My father carried him on his back, my mother and I following behind. At first, we doubled back down the steeper of the two paths, looking for the hidden way my father remembered. There was an atmosphere of neglect, of stillness. And always shouting from down below, the soldiers shouting.

'We had not gone far before we came upon a break in the undergrowth. My father pulled back the twisted and overgrown branches of laurel to reveal ancient roots.'

Fabrissa smiled at the recollection.

'In truth it looked like a flight of steps fashioned from wood, and I said so. Jean was amused at this, so from then on, I concentrated my efforts on keeping him entertained. Distracting him.'

Her face grew serious again.

'But he was coughing almost all the time now. More than once, my father had to gently lower him from his back, and we would wait while Jean struggled to catch his breath.

'At last, we reached a plateau, not much more than a ledge on the mountainside. I could see my father's relief that his memory had not been at fault. Up above I saw a cleft in the rock, in the shape of a half-moon, concealed beneath an overhanging escarpment. From below the plateau, the mouth of the cave was not visible at all. A short tunnel led to a wider space, which connected in turn with a network of caverns deep inside the mountain.

'Then we heard voices, and soon were reunited with our neighbours.'

A sigh escaped from between my lips.

'Each family occupied a small area within which they made their camp. To start with the atmosphere was hopeful. The children played, delighted with the subterranean world, and women helped my mother to nurse Jean. At first, his health improved, and every day he became a little stronger.'

I frowned. 'Every day? How long were you in the caves, then?'

'A long time.'

'Weeks?' I said, appalled at the thought.

'More.' She paused. 'Because it was winter, we had assumed the soldiers would give up and leave us alone until the spring. That was what had happened in the past. And, at the beginning, it seemed to be their intention. They did go, but in the end they always came back. They always came back. It was a game of cat and mouse.'

Fabrissa turned her eyes on me, then back to the wooded horizon. 'We were the last, you see. Our village was one of the few remaining strongholds. They could not let us be. So we waited and we waited. The heavy snows came and we thought they would leave then. But they did not. They occupied the village. Our village.

'The weeks passed. Our spirits began to dwindle. Men left the caves at night to fetch food and more provisions – a little oil for the lamps, candles, kindling to make fires – but it was never enough. Everyone was hungry and cold.'

She hesitated and I, for the first time since she had begun her story, could not stop myself reaching out for her. I tried to take her hands in mine, but her fingers were so cold I could not seem to catch hold of her.

'Jean suffered very badly. The chill and damp got into his bones, his chest. At night, he could not sleep. He coughed continuously, clawing for breath, choking. He needed fresh air and sunlight, the very things we could not give him. Each day, I watched him grow weaker and knew there was nothing I could do. When he died, he was only fourteen years old.'

My heart contracted in pity. That Fabrissa also had lost a beloved brother, but in circumstances so much worse than mine, was more than I could bear. Although my ignorance of the precise circumstances of George's passing had haunted me for years, I'd not had to watch him die. But Fabrissa had been there with Jean. She had seen him slipping from her, unable to do anything to save him. How could anyone live with such memories?

'I'm so very sorry,' I said quietly.

The sun had risen, cold and white in the sky. The black trees and the night-time silhouette of the mountains had transformed into the greens and greys of the new day. I could see snow on the peak of the Roc de Sédour in the distance.

I gathered her to me. This time I held her tight, though she felt insubstantial in my arms, like mist.

'We could not bury him,' she whispered. 'The ground outside was too hard and the floor of the caves was rock. So he was laid with the others who had died: widow Azéma, the Bulot children. Later, many more.'

I caught my breath. For so long, my nights had been haunted by images of George dying in the mud and the blood and the barbed wire, dying with the stench of the charnel house in his nostrils, his men blasted to pieces by mines, by bullets, choked by gas. But to think of Fabrissa trapped in such a place, her beloved Jean dead beside her, this was horror of another dimension.

'It was perhaps a week after he had died, about the

time of the Espéraza winter fair, when we saw ten-drils of smoke rising up above the tree-line. And we knew, then, that the village was burning. Angry they still had not captured us, even though they knew we were somewhere close by, they put everything to the torch. The church, the Ostal, our homes. Everything was destroyed.'

'Fabrissa . . .'

There was nothing more I could say.

'Later, when the thaw began and we had begun to think ourselves forgotten, we became careless. Two men were seen coming back into the caves by night. The soldiers followed and placed a sentinel. Then they found one of the entrances and it was only a matter of time before they found the others.' She paused. 'We heard them, piling up the stones, ham-mering as they braced the rubble with timbers. The light became more shallow, then darkness overcame us. What was a refuge became a tomb. Every open-ing was blocked. We could not get out.'

I felt Fabrissa slide from my arms. I was suddenly dizzy. The nausea I'd managed to keep at bay over-whelmed me.

'No one came back,' she said. 'Not one.'

I feared I was going to pass out. My palms were

clammy and my chest tight. I leaned forward, head down, my arms resting on my legs.

'Freddie?' said Fabrissa. I heard the concern in her voice and loved her for it.

'I'm fine.'

'Freddie,' she whispered, 'do not be afraid.'

'Afraid? I'm not af—'

I jerked my head up, setting colours dancing before my eyes. Heard her lullaby voice saying my name. And this time, I knew without a shadow of a doubt that it had been Fabrissa's voice I had heard through the storm. 'But how?' I murmured. 'How?'

I glanced at her in mute confusion, seeing my own anguish reflected in her face. I was so tired now. I had worn myself out by talking and I realised I was deathly cold.

Fabrissa, too, seemed to be tiring. She did not move, but I sensed a restiveness in her, as if she had already lingered too long. I could feel her slipping away and, much as I wanted to keep her with me, I felt powerless to stop her.

'It's morning,' I said, looking down at the village stirring beneath us. 'I should take you home.'

Sweat was trickling down between my shoulder blades, though I was shaking, frozen right through.

I tried to stand but found that I couldn't. I raised a heavy hand to my forehead. My skin was hot to the touch.

'Perhaps I could see you again?' I tripped over my words. 'Later today. I . . .'

Did I even speak out loud or only in my head?

Again, I tried to get up, but my knees buckled. I slumped back to our makeshift bench, feeling ridges of the bark jabbing into my skin.

'Fabrissa . . .'

It was a struggle to hold my head up. I wanted to free myself, to escape from the prison of my memory.

'I must . . . take you . . . home,' I repeated, but it came out all wrong. I tried to focus on Fabrissa's face, on her grey eyes, but there were two girls now, and the image floated in and out of focus. I tried to say her name again, but the word turned to ashes in my mouth.

'Find me,' she whispered. 'Find us. Then you can bring me home.'

'Fabr—'

Was she leaving me, or was I leaving her? My heart turned in on itself.

'Don't go,' I murmured. 'Please. Fabrissa!'

But she was already too far away. I could not reach her.

'Come and find me,' she whispered. 'Find me, Freddie.'

Then nothing. Only the dreadful knowledge that I was alone once more.

The Fever Takes Hold

'*Monsieur Watson, s'il vous plaît.*'

Someone was calling my name. There was a hand on my shoulder, shaking me. But I did not want to wake.

'Fabrissa . . .'

'*Monsieur Watson.*'

My whole body ached. I was stiff everywhere and unpleasantly conscious of the bones along my left side – ribs, hip-bone, knee-joint – pressing against the hard ground. I swept my right arm in an arc around me and felt dust and wooden floorboards beneath my hand.

I tried to raise my head, but the world spun away from me and I slumped back down. Where was I? Then the same voice, a little louder. Brisk, inviting no argument, like the nurses in the sanatorium.

'*Monsieur, s'il vous plaît, vous devez vous lever.*'

'Fabrissa?' I murmured again.

Again, the hand on my shoulder, strong fingers pressing firmly through to the bone.

Why were they waking me? I didn't need their pills. I didn't want to be awake.

'Leave me alone,' I muttered, trying to turn over.

'You must get up, monsieur. It is not good for you to lie here.'

The woman was not going to go away. I forced my eyes open once more. Instead of white starched uniforms and the black shoes of the ward nurses, I saw a pair of wooden clogs.

Madame Galy. Not the sanatorium, but the boarding house in Nulle. And for some reason I couldn't immediately fathom, I was lying on the floor. I struggled to push myself into a sitting position, dragging my legs round from under me, then tried to stand.

'Let me help you, monsieur.' Madame Galy's strong hand was under my elbow, guiding me to the chair. 'Here.'

I slumped down and leaned forward, elbows on my knees, waiting for the spinning to stop.

'Is she here?'

'Is who here, monsieur?'

'Fabrissa,' I said, my voice rising a little. 'Did she come back with me? Is she here?'

'There is no one else here,' she replied. I could detect confusion behind the kindness.

'She's not here?' A wave of disappointment seeped into me, like ink through blotting paper, though I told myself it was only to be expected. She would be home in bed by now, of course she would. A glass of white liquid appeared under my nose.

'Drink this.'

I'd only taken a couple of bitter sips before my fingers started to shake. Madame Galy's firm, warm hands cupped around mine and helped me to finish. Then she gently removed the glass from me.

'It will help you sleep.'

I nodded, having long ago lost the habit of asking what this pill did or what that medicine might achieve.

'What time is it?'

'Ten o'clock, monsieur.'

'In the morning?'

'Yes.'

I looked around the room. Clearly, it was morning. Everything was bathed in a flat, white light. The fire had burned out, leaving a pyramid of soft, grey ash in the grate. On the hearth, the bottle and glass, both empty.

'We were concerned when you did not come down to breakfast, monsieur.'

'I had no idea it was so late.'

I frowned, trying to get the sequence of events clear in my mind. I'd taken a bath, come back to the room to enjoy a cigarette and a drink while I got ready. I looked down at my clothes. I was wearing the tunic and my tweeds, but of the soft leather boots there was no sign. I could not remember taking them off. I shook my head and a kaleidoscope of colours exploded behind my eyes. I clutched at my temples to control the pain.

'Shall I send for a doctor, monsieur?' Madame Galy said quickly.

'No, no. No doctors.'

The spinning in my head slowed and then finally stopped altogether. Why did I have no memory of leaving Fabrissa and making my way back to the boarding house? I had evidently removed my boots and started to undress, but then what? Had I fainted?

'What time did I come back, do you know?'

'Back, monsieur?'

'From the Ostal? Someone must have heard me.'

There was some quality of caution in her silence, I could tell Madame Galy was struggling with something, perhaps something she wanted to say but dared not.

I wonder how much she knew then about everything that had happened. I was aware that the fever had already taken hold, but I didn't care. All that mattered at that cold moment in the boarding house in Nulle was why Fabrissa was not with me.

Why had she left me?

I leaned back in the chair. What could I remember? The early part of the evening, yes, that was clear. Crossing the place de l'Église, down the alleyway beside the church in the frost. Stars, diamonds in the sky, my fingers cold in my pocket holding the hand-drawn map. Finding the Ostal, Guillaume Marty welcoming me and introducing me to other guests. The heat from the fire and the lilting melody of the troubadour's voice, the ebb and flow of conversation.

And Fabrissa.

I caught my breath. Fabrissa, yes, talking and talking. Laying bare my soul and feeling awkward, but also knowing that my burden had been lightened. And then the trouble had started and the gathering had ended in a brawl. Yes, I remembered that. But we had left, Fabrissa and I, hadn't we, because she told me it would be all right? The memory of the dust and the cobwebs in the tunnel, our hands tearing against splintered wood, then emerging blinking into the tail end of the night on the hillside to the west of the village. And how we sat beside the dewpond as dawn broke, her turn to confide in me. Telling stories of loss and remembrance.

Hadn't we?

I launched myself out of the chair and across the room in a couple of strides. I pulled the windows open, sending the frame banging back against the wall, and thrust myself out as far as I dared. I needed to see the place on the hill where we had sat. Had to prove to myself it was there. Icy air rushed into the room and wrapped itself around me, though I do not believe I could feel it.

I felt Madame Galy's hand on my arm. 'Monsieur, please, come back inside. You will make yourself ill.'

'Up there,' I said, waving in the direction of the rising sun. 'That's where we were.'

I saw the concern in her kind face and was about to reassure her, when I suddenly became aware of the texture of the light in the room. The place de l'Église was covered in a thin dusting of snow.

'When did it start snowing?'

'In the early hours, monsieur. Three or four o'clock.'

I spun round to face her. 'You must be mistaken. It was certainly not snowing when I came in and that was . . .' I stopped, for in truth I could not remember. 'I don't know precisely,' I admitted. 'It was already light.'

It had not been cold enough to snow, I told myself, but my confidence was swiftly eroded. I looked down at my thin, bare arms. My skin was rough with goosebumps and my knuckles, braced tight on the sill, bulged blue.

'It must have been later,' I insisted, pointing down at the pristine snow beneath my window. 'See, no marks. It must have begun to snow after I returned.'

'You should rest, monsieur,' she said gently. It was clear she did not believe me. Discouraged now, I stepped back from the window and allowed her to fasten the windows. The hinges squealed and a sliver of snow fell from the rim to the floor beneath the sill. Then she closed the shutters, too, barricading us against the world. The metal catch fell into place with a rattle.

'You must have heard me come back,' I insisted.

Madame Galy sighed. 'It is not simply a matter of when the snow started,' she said, obviously reluctant to be forced into admitting as much.

'What are you saying?'

She paused, choosing her words with the greatest care. 'Are you certain, monsieur, that you did go out at all? I did not see you at the Ostal last night. None of the other guests saw you. I was worried you had got lost.'

'But that's . . . ridiculous.'

'I concluded that you must have thought better of coming out in the cold. It was only when you did not come down this morning that I began to worry you might be unwell.'

I became aware that I was swaying. Hoping to disguise my unsteadiness, I propped my shoulder against the wall. The paper was old, a repeated pattern of blue and pink meadow flowers, faded in strips where the sun had sucked the colour from it.

'Monsieur, please,' she said. 'You should sit.'

I crossed my arms. 'I quite clearly remember putting on the tunic,' I glanced down, '*this* tunic, and the boots. I left the letter on the counter in reception downstairs, then headed out. Ten o'clock on the button.' I paused. 'Did you find the letter?'

'I did,' she said carefully, 'but I assumed you had left it there, then returned to your room, monsieur. Monsieur Galy says he did not hear you leave.'

I had no answer to that. It was clear she was increasingly concerned for my mental state. Perhaps she thought I was still drunk or suffering the after-effects of yesterday's smash. Her eyes flicked away from mine for an instant, then immediately back as though there was something she did not want me to see. Too late, too slow, mocked the voice in my head. The spiteful voice I had heard so often in the sanatorium, setting me against the doctors and nurses, but had thought I had long since vanquished.

The borrowed boots were lying beneath the table. Had I kicked them off when I'd returned to the room? I could see they were pristine. No evidence that they had been worn outside, certainly not in the snow. The toes had no tell-tale stains of frost or dew. I felt the turn-ups on my trousers. They, too, were dry.

'Look, I remember quite clearly walking to the Ostal.' I spoke slowly, carefully placing one word in front of the other, as a drunk considers each step before taking it. 'I followed your map to the letter. Across the square, along the passageway to the left of the church—'

'The left? You should have gone right.'

I kept talking. 'Well, it served me just as well in the end. I did linger a moment at the crossroads, a bit of a labyrinth in that *quartier* behind the church, as you'd warned me, but pretty soon I got my bearings—'

'Crossroads, monsieur?'

'—and found the Ostal with no difficulty. There was quite a crowd there, everyone dressed up for the *fête*, as you had promised, so it's quite possible, don't you think, that you simply missed me in the crowd.'

Her expression was beginning to alarm me. Sympathetic, but genuinely worried. I had seen such an expression before on the face of the ward sister at the sanatorium on the evening I was admitted.

An inexplicable gulf, now as then, between the logic of my world and of theirs. I steamed on all the same.

'I'm relieved to see you didn't come to any harm in the uproar, Madame Galy. I was worried you might have been hurt.'

'Hurt, monsieur?'

'Fabrissa said not to worry. Part of the tradition of the *fête*, I suppose, but I don't mind telling you, I was taken in. It looked real enough. But, of course, that was much later. Perhaps you had gone already.' I knew I was talking too loudly and too fast, but I couldn't help myself. 'A pleasant chap, by the name of Guillaume Marty, took me in hand, introduced me to . . .' I faltered, trying to recall the names. 'Two sisters, a widow, Na Azéma . . .'

Madame Galy was silent. She had given up trying to reason with me. My confidence cracked a little more.

' . . . and a husband and wife by the name of Authier, yes, and so many of your other neighbours. But most of the evening I spent in the company of a charming girl.' I hesitated, suddenly shy. 'Fabrissa. Do you know her?'

I met Madame Galy's stare and saw pity in her eyes. A sharp memory of Mother that day in the restaurant near Piccadilly, and the contrasting look upon her face. Not pity then, but distaste. I blinked, furious that such a worthless memory, and one of many such, still hurt me.

I tried again.

'A most striking girl, with long dark hair worn loose. Pale complexion. The most astonishing grey eyes. You *must* know her.'

Madame Galy shifted. 'I know no one of that name,' she said.

'Well. Well, maybe she came as someone's guest?'

Before the words were out of my mouth, I knew that was unlikely. If Fabrissa had come with someone else, would she have talked to me all night? Would she have left with me?

'Then again, she might,' I mumbled to myself. 'If she liked me.'

I remembered something else, proof of a kind. 'My coat,' I said vigorously. 'I left it in the lobby of the Ostal. When the brawl started, in my hurry to get us away, I forgot all about it. It must still be there.'

She held her gaze steady. 'Your coat is still hanging on the hook by the front door where I myself hung it up to dry yesterday evening.'

'Well, someone must have brought it back for me,' I shot back, though, in truth, the fight had gone out of me. I couldn't make sense of things. Madame Galy's evidence contradicted my recollection of the evening. What more could be said?

'Fabrissa must have found it and brought it back,' I muttered. Where was she now?

I was shivering. My feet were suddenly painful on the bare floorboards. I wrapped my arms around myself, feeling my ribs beneath the thin tunic.

Madame Galy put her arm around me. 'You should lie down, monsieur.'

'Someone must know her,' I said, though I allowed her to steer me off the chair and towards the bed. She turned away as I took off my trousers, then she lifted the eiderdown and I obediently climbed in. How easily I slipped back into the role of patient. Individual pockets of shiny material hemmed into tight squares of the eiderdown, the colour of nicotine. She pulled it up to my chin, patted it down. Where was Fabrissa? Fragments of our conversation were coming back to me, the awful tragedy of what had happened to her family.

'Was there much enemy activity around here during the War?' I asked.

If Madame Galy was surprised at this change of tack, she did not show it. I realise now, of course, she was humouring me. Like the doctors and nurses in the hospital. Rule One: do nothing to provoke or agitate the patient.

'There was a prison camp near here for prisoners of the Germans at Le Vernet,' she replied, 'but it is some distance from here.'

'I meant rather more along the lines of German units operating in the area? Unofficial action.'

She leaned across me to fuss at the counterpane. Busy, busy hands.

'We lost many of our young men fighting in the north. Monsieur Galy and I . . .' She stopped and, for a moment, before she managed to mask it, raw pain flared in her eyes. To my shame, I did not press her. It was only later I learned what had happened to her. To her family.

'No rogue units?'

'No, monsieur. There was no fighting here.'

I sank back against the bolster. Fabrissa's descriptions of the raid on the village, how they'd all fled into the mountains. Her brother. These were real experiences, vividly remembered.

'So Nulle itself never came under attack? No raid, no evacuation, nothing?'

'No.'

Had I misunderstood? It was possible, certainly. Was it also possible that I had blurred Fabrissa's story with my own? Again, I supposed it was. I closed my eyes. Was I a man who could tell true from false? That's what Fabrissa asked me last evening. Then, I had been sure. But now? Now I was no longer certain the question had even been asked.

'But it is such a sad place,' I heard myself saying. 'When I arrived, I felt there was something, some shadow hanging over the village.'

Madame Galy stopped her housekeeping.

'It was different in the Ostal last night,' I continued. 'There – at least, until the trouble started – everyone seemed in good spirits.'

As if a switch had been flicked, she resumed her fussing. Still she said nothing. She replaced the chair in its position at the table and hung my trousers over the clothes horse.

'Is there anything else you need, monsieur?'

There was nothing I could think of. But I realised I wished she would stay. Her presence was comforting.

'I'm sorry to be such a bother . . .'

'I am happy to do it, monsieur.' She picked up the empty liqueur bottle and glass and put them on the tray. 'I will look in on you in an hour or so,' she said. 'Now you should sleep.'

I was tired, so very tired. Perhaps the sleeping draught she had given me was beginning to take effect.

'When you feel strong enough, Michel Breillac, who knows something of motor cars, is at your disposal. He will help.'

'Thank you,' I murmured, but she had already gone, leaving the door ajar. I listened to the clump of her *sabots* retreating along the passageway and down the stairs. The sound was strangely comforting, ordinary. I lay back against the pillows.

Except for George, the idea of love to me always before seemed a question of submission. Of giving in to some powerful emotion, of losing control. Now love seemed a natural thing, something one did not even need to remark upon, like breathing or raising one's face to the sun on a summer's day.

Fabrissa . . . Like a children's nursery rhyme, her name going round and round in my head. Fabrissa. The word spinning and spiralling and winding my nerves tighter and tighter.

'Where are you?'

I realised I'd spoken it out loud, though it did not matter. There was no one there to hear me.

'I will find you,' I murmured, slipping into sleep with her name still on my lips.

Madame Galy's Vigil

I slept all of that day and into the evening. Or rather, I drifted in and out of a twilight state. I was aware of comings and goings, shapes, blurred faces, the sound of kindling and a striking match, the maid laying a fire.

I woke fully only twice. First, when Madame Galy placed a bowl of soup and bread beside the bed and waited until I had eaten it all. The second time, when she returned to administer a second draught of the bitter white medicine. Some kind of traditional remedy? I never knew and hardly cared.

'What time is it?'

'Late,' she replied, placing a cool hand on my forehead. Why she should take so much trouble over a stranger, I did not think to ask. She felt some kind of responsibility to me, I could see, as a guest in her establishment. Even so, this was over and above the call of duty.

But Madame Galy's maternal ministrations were not enough to stop the fever from taking hold. Some time in the evening, my temperature began to rise dangerously. Every muscle, every sinew flexed and tried to fight it, but my natural defences were too weak and I was powerless to do anything other than hope to ride the fever out.

My skin was alternately burning and clammy with sweat. I tossed and turned in the bed, like flotsam on a storm-wracked sea, plagued by dreams and delusions. Angels and gargoyles, ghostly apparitions, long-since deserted friends waltzed in and out of my head, to the sounds of a fairground carousel, then *Für Elise*, then a ragtime step.

For hours, so Madame Galy later told me, things hung in the balance as my temperature climbed higher and higher. Certainly, I oscillated between beauty and horror. A skeletal hand pushing up from beneath freshly turned earth, blossom dying on the bough. The backs of my parents' heads, impassive and deaf to my need for them to love me. George smiling at me, in the orchard and by the stream, but then stepping just out of reach and turning away when I called out to him. Barbed wire and mud and blood, chlorine gas, a world of unimaginable pain.

The fever broke at about three o'clock in the morning. I felt it slink away like a mongrel with its tail between its legs. My temperature dropped. I stopped shaking and my skin, sticky with fever, returned to normal. For the first time in hours, I found myself surrounded by the reassuringly mundane features of the everyday world. A chair, my trousers draped over a clothes horse, a table, the last lick of flames in the grate and Madame Galy snoring quietly on the chair beside me. Wisps of grey hair had worked their way loose from her severe plait, and I caught a glimpse of the pretty girl she once had been. I could think of no occasion when my own mother had taken such care of me. Without waking her, I reached out my hand and laid it briefly over hers.

'Thank you,' I whispered.

Then a kind of peace fell over the room. In the still and sleeping house, I could hear the whirring and chiming of the clock in the hall downstairs. I placed my arms above the counterpane, a stone knight on a tomb, and turned to the window. I wondered if Fabrissa looked out into the same night. I wondered if she might have come to enquire after me. I had set at her feet what little of myself I had to give, ragged fragments, and yet hoped that she might love me. Had it scared her off? Was she lying awake now in the dark, thinking of me as I thought of her?

A ribbon of moonlight made its way between the shutters and painted a line across the floor. I watched the moonbeams dance, slowly shift, as the hours passed and the world continued to turn. I thought of what I would say to her when I found her. Of the beauty of small things. Of the way a bird takes flight, its wings beating on the air. Of the blue flowers of the flax blossom in summer and a parish church decorated by plough and corn at harvest time. Of notes climbing a chromatic scale. Of the possibility of love.

Later, I fell asleep. And this time, when I slept, I did so without dreaming.

*

When I woke again, it was morning. Madame Galy had gone. The chair was back against the wall as if it had never been moved. Physically, I was done in, but I felt all right – in fact, better than I had for some time. And I was ravenously hungry.

I sat up, debating whether to get up or wait a while

longer. I wasn't certain of the time. Just as I had decided that I would wash and dress, there was a light
tap on the door.

'Come in.'

Madame Galy came into the room, my laundered
shirt over her arm, and carrying a breakfast tray.

'I have brought you something to eat,' she said.

I smiled and smoothed down the covers.

'That's kind of you. I seem to have quite an appetite
this morning.'

I was touched by the way she found things to busy
herself with in the room, while surreptitiously check-
ing that I ate every scrap. Toasted bread, salted ham
and an egg sliced perfectly in two. When I tried to
thank her for her long night's vigil, she brushed my
gratitude aside. But a pink glow suffused her homely
features and I could see she was pleased.

'Your letter was delivered to your friends in Ax
yesterday afternoon, monsieur. The boy can go again
tomorrow once you know how things stand with
your motor car.'

'Thank you.' I wiped my hands on the serviette.
'You said there was someone who could help?'

She nodded. 'Michel Breillac and his sons will be
here at ten o'clock.'

'What time is it now?'

'It is nearly nine.'

'Splendid. I can easily be ready within an hour.'

Concern flashed across Madame Galy's face when she realised I intended to accompany them.

'I do not think it would be wise, monsieur, after what you went through last evening. It is barely above freezing. Better to give Monsieur Breillac directions and leave it to him. He is a capable man.'

It seems extraordinary now that I would have contemplated an expedition after so serious a fever. But in truth, I believed the delirium had left me somehow stronger, restored. I felt invigorated, more complete in body and mind than I had been for some time.

'I'm quite recovered,' I said with a smile. 'On top form, in fact.'

She shook her head. 'It would be better to rest for one more day. You should not overtire yourself.'

'It will be fine,' I said firmly.

Supervising the salvage of my poor little saloon stranded up in the hills was not, of course, my primary concern. Madame Galy said she did not know Fabrissa, so I had to find someone who did. That could not be achieved by kicking my heels in the boarding house.

'Very well, monsieur,' she said, though I could see she thought me foolish. 'Ten o'clock.'

After she had left, I flung back the covers and got out of bed. The floorboards were chill beneath my bare feet, but the ground held steady. I splashed cold water on my face and did my best to smooth down my errant hair. I ran my hand over my raspy chin and regretted the lack of a razor, but did not want to seek out Madame Galy once more, for fear she would renew her efforts to dissuade me from accompanying the Breillacs.

I finished dressing and pulled on my Fitwells. The leather of the sturdy old boots had contracted in the heat from the fire, but they were comfortable enough. I rummaged in my trouser pocket and retrieved my cigarette case and matches, then threw open the windows and looked out at the white place de l'Église.

I plunged my hand back into my pocket. Nothing. I balanced my cigarette on the sill. I frowned. After I had offered the yellow fabric cross to Fabrissa and she had refused it, I could have sworn I'd tucked it away. I tried the other pocket, but it was also empty. Just balls of fluff and a spent match.

Had I mislaid it on the way home? Since I had no recollection at all of how I had made it back to my room, it seemed the likeliest explanation, though I was disappointed.

'No matter,' I said to myself, shutting the window.

I was certain, you see, that I would find her.

The Breillac Brothers

As the last chime of the clock struck ten, I came downstairs to the reception area.

Monsieur Breillac and his two sons were already there, and introductions were quickly made. Guillaume and Pierre Breillac were twins, of eighteen or nineteen or so, their faces all but hidden by fur hats tied beneath the chin. In any event, they looked so similar I found it hard to tell them apart, until it became evident that Guillaume spoke passable English, whereas Pierre did not. Monsieur Breillac said nothing, just nodded a greeting, and I detected the same sadness in his eyes that clouded Monsieur Galy's, Madame Galy's too when she thought no one was watching.

She was still adamant I should not go, but when she saw I would not be deflected, found me a fur hat and muffler to wear as well as a pair of heavy men's gloves.

'Please thank Monsieur Galy for the loan,' I said. 'They're a perfect fit.'

'They are not my husband's,' she said quietly. I saw a look pass between the Breillac boys and their father, but nobody said anything, so I threaded my fingers into the soft fur lining without further comment and thought no more about it.

Guillaume acted as interpreter, because although my French was adequate, it did not stretch to such technicalities as torque tube or running board. With a mixture of hand gestures and his blunt translation, we established where the car might be and what I considered the extent of the damage.

We set off shortly after ten-fifteen under a blue sky, unbroken by clouds. As we crossed the place de l'Église, I felt my heart expand with the beauty of it; the same old world, but seen through new eyes. A white winter sun hung low in the sky and it was bright but cold.

Monsieur Breillac put his hand on Guillaume's arm and spoke rapidly in patois. I waited until he translated. His father suggested we should climb up through the woods rather than risk the *charreton*. A two-person cart pulled by a donkey, he explained in response to my raised eyebrows. His father said the road would be iced over and it would be slow and treacherous going. Whereas the woodland paths, protected by the trees, would be more secure underfoot. If I had the stamina for it, that was.

Having been so wretchedly ill, you might wonder at my arrogance. Or stupidity, I suppose. Indeed, I wonder at it myself, even now. Looking back, though, I can only say that I knew I had the strength I needed. The fever had passed through me, leaving in its place a kind of nervous energy and a sense of purpose I'd been lacking for some time.

I readily agreed to Breillac's proposal. And I was excited, too. Sitting beside the dewpond, Fabrissa had invited me to come and find her. And it was in these mountains that I had first heard her voice.

There had been no fresh snow overnight so, despite a hard frost, the going was not too bad. We walked at a fair pace and soon arrived at the bridge which I had crossed two days previously. As we tramped over it, the Billy Goats Gruff and I, the frozen water below glinted in the December morning like the surface of a looking-glass. Reeds and brown rushes stuck up through the ice like a line of tin soldiers, as if caught at the precise moment the winter took hold.

We walked across the drab fields, the brown furrows crusted with snow, and were soon on the outskirts of the woods where the trees sparkled with frost.

I pointed out the path by which I had descended and, in single file, we began to climb. It was steep, yet it seemed less taxing than previously. Breillac and his sons were easy company, and the sun and the lack of wind lifted my spirits. I kept my ears peeled for Fabrissa's voice, but today there was no suggestion of figures in the mist or watchers in the hills.

I held off asking the Breillacs if they knew of Fabrissa because I did not want my hopes dashed. The longer I delayed the question, the longer I kept the possibility alive that they could tell me where to find her.

So on we went. I remember a bird singing high up in the barren branches of a tree. A hen blackbird, maybe a robin, oddly English sounds to hear in a French country wood, prompting the absurd thought that Fabrissa and I might, some day, walk hand in hand on the Sussex Downs. My plans were castles in the air, of course, dreams, imaginings of silver days we might spend in one another's company. The countless dusks watching the sun sinking down into the earth. The nights in one another's arms. And I smiled as I remembered her clever grey eyes and the pale turn of her chin and the drape of her hair across her shoulders. My heart ached to see her again.

'I wonder, Guillaume, if you might know a girl by the name of Fabrissa?'

He thought for a moment, then shook his head.

'What about Pierre? Perhaps your father. Could you ask?' He turned around and I, keeping my tone light, carried on chattering, shoring up my defences against disappointment. 'We were introduced at the fête, a couple of nights ago. Like an idiot, I didn't catch her last name. Be interested to know where she lives.'

I heard Breillac repeat her name, but he was shaking his head, and so was Pierre. Guillaume turned back to face me. 'No,' he reported, 'they don't know of such a girl.' Then he added, 'My father says he didn't see you, monsieur, at the Ostal.'

My stomach gave an unpleasant lurch.

'He didn't?' I paused. 'Well, it was crowded. Hard to see anyone much. I didn't even catch a glimpse of Madame Galy all night and it was she who'd invited me. The way of these things, I suppose.' I paused. 'Your father didn't get caught up in the brawl?' I gave a brittle laugh. 'Do you know, I thought it was real to start with. Those swords and helmets, very convincing.'

Guillaume's eyes cut into me. 'Brawl, monsieur?'

'The fight, then,' I said. 'The punch-up.' I stopped and looked at him. 'You were there, Guillaume? The *fête de Saint-Etienne*?'

'I was. We all were.'

Guillaume was genuinely baffled and I, feeling I had somehow blotted the day for us all, said nothing more. But it preyed on my mind. Even admitting I was rather preoccupied at the time, it was queer that my recollection of the evening was so at odds with theirs.

We walked on, barely talking as the path grew steeper yet. At last, I made out the junction where the two paths became a single track leading back up to the road.

We stopped to catch our breath. It was then that I felt the familiar prickling at the nape of my neck, the same thickening of the air. I glanced up into the dense undergrowth to my left and, in the gloom, made out the gnarled roots of some ancient trees, vanishing into the mountain.

'Like stairs,' I murmured, hearing Fabrissa's voice in my head.

'Monsieur, it is this way, yes?'

'What?'

I realised my three companions had stopped and were waiting on me for further directions.

'That's right, yes. Straight on.'

An Idea Takes Hold

It was close to eleven-thirty when we emerged from the path by the wooden sign.

We halted a while to rest. I offered my cigarettes, and Breillac senior passed round a canteen of a foul, aniseed-flavoured liqueur. Each of us took a swig, then wiped it off with our gloves before passing it on.

The atrocious weather conditions of two days ago, and my disorientation immediately after the smash, meant I couldn't estimate with any accuracy how much further along the road I was when the accident happened. In the event, we walked for no more than five minutes before the yellow Austin came into view.

'*Voilà*,' I shouted, relieved to see that my motor car had not toppled over completely. '*Voilà la voiture.*'

Half skating up the icy road, half walking, it took no more than a minute or two to cover the last couple of hundred yards. The four of us stared at the yellow car, Breillac and his sons talking too fast for me to follow.

I watched Guillaume take the coil of rope from around his shoulder and tie it to the rear bumper. He then looped it around his waist, and Pierre followed suit. They braced their knees and began to pull, Breillac standing by and hollering like a barker at the fish market.

With the scraping of metal on the hard ground and grunts from the boys, the car was slowly dragged back from the edge of the precipice until all four wheels were back on *terra firma*.

'Splendid,' I said, nodding to Guillaume. '*Et à vous, Pierre, merci.*'

Guillaume untied the rope, then stood back to allow Breillac a clear view. He walked around the battered little car as if he were at an auction, shaking his head as he pointed at the axle, at the buckled front wheel arch, at some indeterminate piece of cable that hung down like a torn thread. His expression alone announced it was going to be difficult to fix.

'*Quatre, cinq jours, minimum.*'

'He says—'

'Four or five days, yes. Can you ask him what he

thinks we should do now? Is there a garage in Nulle? Or do we need to think about getting it towed to Tarascon?'

Guillaume turned to his father to start up another lengthy discussion, so I removed myself a little way from their loud voices and sat on a rock. The sun had risen over the mountain and it was, if not actually warm, then at least not properly cold. There was the odd snatch of birdsong, and the air was filled with the smell of pine resin.

I shielded my eyes against the lacy glare of the white sun on the mountains and scanned the slopes below the road. There were no houses, no signs of human habitation that I could see. Guillaume confirmed it. Apart from the shepherds' huts, deserted in winter, no one lived this high in the valley. It was too harsh an environment, too bitterly cold and exposed.

I lit a cigarette, thinking of what Fabrissa had said. The path along which she and her family had travelled was overgrown with box and . . . and what? I drummed my fingers on my knee, box leaves and . . . I got it.

'Silver birch. Evergreen box trees and silver birch.'

Both were common in this part of France, but I could see both from where I was sitting. The distinctive silver and black markings of a cluster of birch trees and, a little to the right of them, the deep green of box shrubs. Confirmation, surely, I was on the right track?

'And maybe where I'll find her . . .'

'Monsieur?' said Guillaume, a quizzical look on his face.

I flushed. 'Thinking aloud,' I said, getting to my feet. 'What news? What does your father suggest?'

I tried to pay attention as Guillaume outlined Breillac's plan, but my thoughts kept slipping back to the patch of earth below us.

' . . . if that is agreeable to you, monsieur. If not, we will find another way.'

I realised Guillaume had stopped talking and was looking at me.

'Forgive me. I didn't catch that. Could you . . . ?'

Guillaume began again in his slow, steady voice.

'As my father sees it, there are two . . .'

Out of the corner of my eye I saw something move in the valley below. A flash of blue, perhaps. I couldn't tell. I took a step forward and, using the tips of the bare branches of the silver birch as my sight-line, traced a direct line to the hillside on the opposite side of the valley. I narrowed my gaze and hit upon an overhang of grey rock, sheltered by trees. There seemed to be a shelf in the rock and, though it was hard to make out, perhaps an opening, in the shape of an eyebrow.

'. . . so given the damage to the chassis,' Guillaume concluded, 'my father thinks it is a job for a trained mechanic. An old colleague of his works chez Fontez in Tarascon, so he could get you a good price.'

'Is it possible to get up over there?' I pointed south-east at the opposite escarpment.

If Guillaume was offended by my inattention, he didn't show it.

'If you keep straight on this road, then drop down near Miglos. Though I don't know why anyone would want to. There's nothing there.'

'What about from this side of the valley? From here? Is there a path up through these woods?'

'If there is, I don't know of it.' He shrugged. 'There was mining in that section of the mountains, before my time, to open up a new route south. Twenty years ago. It changed the shape of the land and the hills.' He paused. 'So it is possible there is a path, but it would be a hard climb.'

'Yes, it would,' I murmured, thinking of a courageous girl and a boy too ill to walk far.

Guillaume shifted his weight from foot to foot, impatient to get things set. 'About the car, monsieur, should we take it to Tarascon? That is acceptable to you?'

Now I knew – suspected – Fabrissa's cave was there, I couldn't concentrate on anything else. I dragged my eyes away from the shelf of rock just long enough to tell Guillaume the proposal was fine.

He sighed and gave a thumbs-up sign to his father.

'Pierre can wait here with the car while I go to Tarascon to make the arrangements. Father will guide you back to Nulle.'

I hesitated. 'Actually, Guillaume, do you know what, I think I'll stay here with the car.'

Guillaume's eyes grew round. 'But it will be a long wait, monsieur,' he objected. 'Pierre is happy to remain and keep watch. He is accustomed to the air up here. You should return to the village.'

'No, I insist,' I said.

'But what will you do?'

'I'll find something to do to amuse myself. Read a book. I'll wait in the car if the cold starts to get to me.' I gave an impatient nod. 'You go on. The sooner you get going, the sooner you'll be back.'

Although far from happy, Guillaume realised there

was little he could do. He explained to his father and brother. For the first time, Breillac spoke directly to me in the old language of the region, in a voice that resonated with tobacco and old age.

'I'm sorry, I don't understand.'

A look passed between the brothers, then Guillaume spoke again to his father, before translating for me once more.

'He is anxious you should not stay. This is a bad place for you to be, he says. An unhappy place.'

'Oh, come along.' I smiled. 'Tell your father I appreciate his concern, but I'll be fine.'

Breillac stared at me with eyes as hard as buttons.

'Trèvas,' he growled, jabbing at me with his finger. 'Fantaumas.'

I turned to Guillaume. 'What's he saying?'

He flushed. 'That there are spirits in these mountains.'

'Spirits.'

'*E'l Cerç bronzís dins las brancas dels pins. Mas non. Fantaumas del ivèrn.*'

Breillac's words were vaguely familiar, though I couldn't place them. I turned again to Guillaume.

'He says that although they sing of the Cers wind crying in the trees when the snows come, it is the voices of those trapped in the mountains.' He hesitated. 'The winter ghosts.'

A shiver crept down my spine. For a moment, we stood motionless, each wondering what the others might do. Then I clapped my hands together, as at the punchline to a splendid joke, and laughed. The spell Breillac's words had cast over us was broken. I refused to be scared by an old man's superstitions. And Guillaume and Pierre laughed, too.

'I'll keep an eye out,' I said, slapping Guillaume on the back. 'Tell your father not to worry. You get off now. Tell him I'll be here waiting, no question of it.'

Breillac fixed me with a hard stare and the intensity of it shook me a little, I don't mind admitting. But he said nothing more, and after a moment, he turned and beckoned for his sons to follow.

I stood in the middle of the road watching as they grew smaller and smaller. Guillaume and Pierre, steady, sure-footed giants; their father a small, wiry figure walking between them, his shoulders rounded, as if bowed down by the years.

The sight of them moved me. It can't have been regret, for one cannot mourn what one has never had. The Breillacs were a family. They belonged to one another. I had never experienced that. I'd been connected to my parents by a shared surname and an address, but nothing more than that. I couldn't recall a single occasion when George, my father and I had done anything together, even taken a simple walk over the Downs from Lavant to East Dean.

George had been my family. He, alone, had loved me. I stopped as another thought marched into my mind. I smiled. Perhaps, in time, Fabrissa might come to love me. The idea shimmered for a moment, glorious and bright, then burst like a firework on Guy Fawkes Night.

Filled with renewed determination to find her, I strode back to the car. I leaned across from the driver's seat and retrieved my rubber torch from the glove compartment. My Baedeker was still lying on the passenger seat, its pages swollen with the damp and snow blown in through the broken windscreen. I shook it out of the door to loosen the fragments of glass stuck in the crease of the spine, then studied the map. This time I found Nulle. A tiny dot on the map, the name was buried in the fold of the pages. It was hardly surprising I'd missed it before.

I located Miglos, the village Guillaume had mentioned earlier, and traced a triangle with my finger to fix my route. I frowned. The distances on the map, and what I could see with my own eyes, did not appear to match up. I realised why that might be. Guillaume said there had been mining in the area – quarrying, I presumed – twenty years ago. That would account for certain differences. I flicked to the front of the Baedeker and found this edition had been printed in 1901.

Aware I was wasting time I could not spare, I decided to use the sun as my guide. Once I was on the far side of the valley, I had faith that the bright yellow paintwork of my Austin would mark my starting point.

What else did I need? I was warm enough in the borrowed fur hat and gloves, but my Fitwells were not designed for such terrain and I'd slipped many times on the climb up here. I twisted round and reached over the seat for my suitcase. I fumbled with the metal clasps until they flipped open, and hooked out my hiking boots. As I did so, my fingers brushed against cold metal.

Placing the boots on the ground outside the car, I turned back and thrust my hand in amongst the hotchpotch of clothes and paperback books until I found the revolver.

I leaned back in the seat and stared at the Webley.

It wasn't loaded and I had no ammunition with me. I could picture the squat cardboard box in the top drawer of my rented lodgings in Chichester. I wondered if it had been a gesture of self-preservation to leave the bullets behind, but now even the question seemed superfluous. The gun was no use to me and would only weigh me down.

I put it back and closed the case. I changed my boots, then, armed only with my rubber torch, I got out of the car and shut the door.

I felt invincible and full of resolve, almost lightheaded with it. Fabrissa had taken up residence in every corner of my mind and heart. She was present in every breath I took, in every thought. What I would do once I found the cave – if I found it – did not come into it.

Looking back, it seems ludicrous that I could have been so convinced by a glimpse of blue seen across the valley, but in truth it did not cross my mind that it could be anyone but Fabrissa. She had told me to find her and I would keep my word. Such naivety, such delusion.

But such wonderful hope.

The Cave Discovered

I made my way back to the signpost and entered the forest once more, feeling like a boy playing truant from school.

The atmosphere felt different. It was partly because there was no mist and the sunlight filtered down through the canopy of mostly bare branches, scattering patches of gold upon the path. But it was also because, thanks to its association now with Fabrissa, I felt at home. I felt part of the landscape, welcome in it, no longer an intruder.

Now I knew where I was going, I covered the ground quickly. Soon I was standing at the place where the twisted roots were visible beneath the scrub. I took a deep breath and began to pull at the undergrowth. It was dense and matted and the frost held everything in its sharp grip. But the fur-lined gloves, although cumbersome, provided good protection, and after a few sharp tugs I managed to pull back a branch, releasing the aroma of damp earth. Sure enough, it revealed a staircase of roots snaking up through the deep evergreen, just as Fabrissa had said.

Bracing my foot against the slope, I kept pulling, a lone contestant in a tug-of-war, until the branch came loose enough for me to duck underneath. I began to climb, hands on my thighs, locking my muscles with each step, like Mallory and Irvine on Everest, going for the top. The roots were slippery and unsafe, and I stumbled onto my hands and knees several times. The steps grew further and further apart, and steeper, too, until in the end it was more like climbing a ladder that twisted all the way up the mountain.

I began to tire. It was exhausting work, always bent double, and I could not imagine how Fabrissa and Jean had managed it in the dead of night and in fear of their lives. But they had. And so could I.

Just when I had reached the limits of my endurance and thought I could go no further, I found myself in the open. I straightened up and stretched my cramped shoulders and arms, then perched on a boulder for a moment to catch my breath and take stock of my surroundings.

I was in a glade, ringed by trees. Although it wasn't the plateau I had spied from the road, it wasn't far from it. I recognised the green circle of leaves and branches, like a May Queen's crown. Behind me, I could just make out the splash of yellow of my motor car on the grey road. My base camp. And above me, like gaping mouths in the rock face, was a series of openings beneath the jutting escarpments.

I plucked a few stray twigs and branches from my coat, tossed them to the ground, then stood up and prepared to go on.

Did it worry me that there were no signs of human habitation? No wisps of smoke visible? Not even a shepherd's hut? Certainly no evidence of a village or hamlet? I don't think it did. At that moment, all I could think about was how I was going to make it to the summit in one piece.

I continued to climb, my thighs shrieking in complaint. Each step was purgatory, an act of endurance, but I found my rhythm and stuck to it. Head down, shoulders forward, knees braced. Sweat trickled down the back of my neck beneath the heavy fur hat, though I knew better than to remove it. My fingers were swimming inside the gloves and my toes were prickly inside my woollen socks and hiking boots. Everything hurt.

But I made it. Now I was directly below the cleft in the rock. From this vantage point, the caves looked to be natural, not man-made, though I was too far away to be certain. A few appeared large enough to harbour a man standing upright. Others only just sufficient for a child to squeeze inside on his hands and knees.

Once I got close enough to see it properly, the beauty of the place took what little breath remained in my lungs. The wind and the rain, the heat and cold, had sculpted the rock over thousands of years. At first glance, it reminded me of photographs I'd seen of tombs in the Holy Land, of the tragedy at Masada. But here in the Ariège, everything was green and grey and brown beneath the dusting of snow, rather than the yellow of the desert.

I glanced at the sky. Counting back from the time at which Breillac and his boys had left me, I estimated it must be somewhere around one o'clock. Time enough.

I walked slowly along the ridge, peering into the hollows and battling down a seeping sense of disappointment. None of them could be the cave within which Fabrissa and her family had taken shelter. Most only went back a yard or two. Nor was there anywhere for her to hide now.

Then I noticed a ribbon of grass, winding up between the rocks. Leaning my shoulder against the side of the mountain to anchor myself, and trying not to think about what would happen if I fell, I edged towards it. Just a few more steps. Don't look down, Freddie, don't look down. And then I saw, directly above my head, an overhang of grey rock, like a protruding lip. Beneath it was an opening the shape of a half moon.

Dizzy with relief, I leaned against the broad flank of the mountain and allowed my heart to settle. I'd done it. I mustered my strength to cover the last few feet and, finally, I was there. Fabrissa's cave.

What was I thinking then? Did I think she would be inside waiting for me, like a game of hide-and-seek at a party? Or perhaps, like a treasure hunt, that there would be secreted in the cave some kind of a clue as to where I should go next? I can't remember. I can only recall my pride at having faced down the challenge and the exquisite anticipation at the thought of seeing Fabrissa again. For I did still believe she was there, somewhere, trusting me to find her.

'Fabrissa?' I called out, but only my own voice answered in the echo.

I peered into the darkness of the cave. At its highest point the opening was about four feet high and five or six feet wide. I turned over a stone with the tip of my boot. The surface was touched with snow but the damp soil beneath was alive with worms and beetles. As my eyes adjusted to the gloom, the short hairs rose on the back of my neck. This was the right cave, I was sure of it. But I felt a sense of apprehension. One could say a premonition. Something was not quite right. I ignored it. I wasn't going to turn back now.

I slipped the torch from my pocket. The beam was weak, suggesting the battery was low, but it cast a useful light. I lowered my head and stepped inside. It was cool and damp in the entrance but, if anything, a little warmer than outside. I shone the torch around, sending shadows dancing along the jagged grey walls as I edged slowly forward. The ground sloped down beneath my feet, gritty and uneven. Loose stones and small pieces of rock crunched beneath my boots. The daylight grew faint at my back.

Suddenly, I was forced to stop, unable to go another step further. A wall of stone and rubble, braced by a carapace of wood, blocked the passage. Holding the torch higher, I ran my eyes over the obstruction. Rubble held tightly in place by timbers. And, with a gnawing unease, I remembered what Fabrissa had said as we sat beside the dewpond, though it had barely registered at the time: no one came back. Not one.

I pulled at one of the struts of wood. I expected resistance, but it crumbled to powder in my hands. I pulled at another piece and it too came easily free, crumbling in my fist, eaten away by woodworm or termites. Beating down a rising sense of panic, I propped my torch on a stone ledge and attacked the wall. The gloves were too thick to get between the tiny cracks in the facade, so I tossed them aside, the hat, too, and clawed at the rubble with my bare hands.

I don't know how long I worked, dislodging one stone, then another. The tips of my fingers were bleeding and my upper arms ached, but I was possessed by a wild need to know what lay behind the barricade. Dust billowed into the narrow passageway as I worked.

Finally, there was an opening as big as my hand. I kept going, using rocks as tools to chip away at the hole, then reached my arm in as far as my shoulder and heaved until it was wide enough for me to get through.

I took a deep breath, steeling myself, I suppose, to cope with whatever might be to come, then clambered into the prison of rock and stone.

Bones and Shadows and Dust

Straight away, the smell of air long undisturbed hit me, musty and expectant after its long confinement.

After a few paces, the tunnel curved a little to the left, then immediately opened out into an extraordinary, soaring cavern, the dimensions of a cathedral. In awe at the sheer scale of it, I shone the torch at the walls and up above my head. The beam vanished into the darkness.

'A city in the mountains,' I muttered.

For a moment, a feeling of calm came over me, a kind of peace to be in so ancient a place. Their refuge, she'd called it. A refuge that became a tomb.

A long sigh of relief escaped from between my lips. There was nothing to see. Until that moment, I did not realise how much I'd started to fear what I might find.

Fabrissa could not be here. It had taken me long enough to break down the obstruction and it seemed unlikely there would be another way in.

'But then where are you?' I whispered into the silence, at last facing what common sense had told me all along. I shook my head. I'd felt so sure I would find her. And, in truth, I somehow felt her presence at my side. Somewhere close by.

I shone the torch around the cave, sending the beam darting into every crevice. Suddenly, I stopped. Something had struck a discordant note. Taking a step forward, I directed the light towards a protrusion of grey rock emerging at forty-five degrees from the wall. There was something on the ground beside it. I moved forward, keeping the torch steady, until I saw it was a sheet of paper, lying as if impossibly blown there by a sudden gust of wind.

I picked it up. It was rough to the touch, a coarse weave. Parchment rather than vellum or the page of a book, much like the cheap papyrus tourists brought back with them from Cook's tours of Ancient Egyptian sites. I opened it out. It was covered in scratchy, old-fashioned handwriting, more like music on a stave than printed letters. I could not read it, even when I held the parchment right up to the light.

I folded it and put it in my pocket. There would be time enough to decipher it later.

Looking up, I noticed a fissure in the rock face directly ahead. Shining the torch in front of me, I went to investigate. There was a narrow corridor, a black seam between two massive ribs of the mountain. It was exceedingly narrow and there was no way of telling how long it was, nor where it went. I felt claustrophobic merely looking at it.

But I forced myself to go in. Holding the torch above my head, I inched my way through, sideways on.

'Take it steady,' I said, hating the rock pressing on my shoulders. 'Steady now.'

In the event, the conduit wasn't so long, and after only a few paces it opened out into a small, self-contained chamber. Unlike the barren outer cave, here was evidence this cavern had been occupied. In the gloom, I could make out a few belongings, the remains of a camp, what might once have been blankets, a snatch of blue and maybe grey, hard to tell the difference in the yellow light of the torch.

'Fabrissa?'

Why did I call her name once more? I'd already

decided she could not be there. But I called out to her all the same, as though a part of me even now hoped she might be there waiting for me.

I walked closer. The torch picked out fragments of red cloth, green and grey and brown. An earthenware bowl and the stump of a tallow candle burnt down to the wick.

My pulse sped up. My subconscious mind knew what I was seeing, but I could not yet let myself face it head on. I could not accept it. Did not want to accept it.

There was something else now, an acrid smell. Like in church, when the congregation has departed but the scent of stale incense from the thurible has not yet faded. I dug in my pocket for my handkerchief and slapped it over my nose and mouth. It reeked of dried blood and oil, but even that did not completely mask the smell of the cave.

Then I heard it. The whispering. But this time, a multitude, not a single voice, the words layered one upon the other like plainsong at vespers, the harmony holding in the echo.

I stared around. There was nothing to see. Nothing moving in the shadows. Nothing. But the whispering was all around me now, behind, in front, above, a sibilance of voices weeping and calling, desperate to be heard.

'*We are the last, the last.*'

'Where are you?' I cried. 'Show yourselves.'

I stumbled forward, nausea rising in my throat. I was being drawn to the furthest corner of the cavern. I did not want to go, but I could not turn back.

Now another voice. Clearer. Distinct. Intended for my ears only.

'*Bones and shadows and dust.*'

'Fabrissa?' I called out into the darkness.

I staggered on, closer to the epicentre of the sound, until my feet came to a halt of their own accord.

I needed to go no further. I didn't want to, but I made myself look. Made myself focus on what I knew I did not wish to see. I was standing in a city of bones, men and women and children, all lying side by side, as if they had lain down to sleep and forgotten to wake.

I bowed my head, my eyes smarting, undone by the sight of the humble objects, treasures. Candles, cooking utensils, a pitcher lying on its side. Grave goods for those who had no more need of them.

At last, my head acknowledged what my heart had told me all along. Now I understood the story

Fabrissa had told me, though I had not wanted to hear it before.

Had not been able to hear before.

Here were fragments of the long green robe of Guillaume Marty, scraps of something still attached to the leather belt around his waist. Here, the royal-blue robes with red stitching, rags now, worn by the Maury sisters. Here, a remnant or two of Na Azéma's grey veil pulled up over her face. No longer people, but skeletons. Skulls half-concealed by a hood or a fold of material or by shadow, the bones glowing green-white in the pale beam of my torch.

Swallowing down the bile rising in my throat, I walked on. Now I could see the bones were clustered in groups, where families had died together. How many bodies lay here entombed? Fifty people. A hundred? More? Had anyone escaped this living death? Fabrissa said no one came back. A refuge that became a tomb. A mass tomb for the people of Nulle.

But the worst was to come. The whispering was getting louder, the pleading, crying for someone to help them. Begging for release. And joined now by another sound, superimposed on the whispering. A scratching on the stone. The rattle of bone on the rough and uneven ground. I wanted to turn back, but

I could not. I could not look away for to do so would be to abandon them once more. I could not stop my ears against the horror of the voices.

I had not yet found Fabrissa, and though I prayed against all the odds that I would not, I knew it was only a matter of time. Her voice singing in the mountains, in the Ostal, the syllables and vowels smudged and indistinct, everything led to the same conclusion.

The noise intensified. Screaming now, a desperate clawing at rock and stone that could not be shifted. Not the Cers wind but, as old Breillac had said, the spirits of the dead. For countless years, the village of Nulle had lived in the shadow of the memories held in this ancient forest.

I could see shapes in the darkness, shifting and sighing, surrounding me. They would not let me be. The cave was full of movement. White shadows, sketches in the air, the silhouette of souls of the dead departed. I covered my face with my hands, knowing it would make no difference. The black parade would walk before me all the same. As I had heard them die, so too was I condemned to watch them die.

Faces loomed in and out of my vision, a terrible beauty in their eyes, coming closer, then withdrawing. Those whom I had met in the Ostal, greeting me once more. Familiar strangers. The man who had sat beside me scowling, his skull now pushing through the skin. In place of his drunken eyes, hollow sockets the size of a man's thumb. In place of his greasy mouth, emaciated lips and blackened teeth. The gentle face of Na Azéma, almost puzzled as her features slipped away from her, leaving nothing but white bone and the memory of whom she had been.

I knew why I had been brought here. I had been brought to bear witness, both to the manner of their dying and to the nature of the prison I'd fashioned for myself.

Without understanding, there can be no redemption. And at that moment it made perfect sense to me how I, a man who for so many years had walked the line between the quick and the dead, might be able to hear their voices in the silence when others could not. For ten years, I'd heard and sensed things that lay beyond the boundaries of the everyday. I'd been haunted by images of George taken back into the earth. Now, in this place, I was witnessing skin slipping from bone, the putrefaction of flesh, the cavalcade of life and death and decay accelerated. Each feature twisting in upon itself, rotting, collapsing. Lives lived, lives lost. Cradle to grave.

It was too much to bear. I was aware of a different sound, one all too human. The sound of a grown man weeping. At last, I was crying. For George, for myself. For all those who lay forgotten in the cold earth.

Then I felt it. A sudden shift, a thickening of the air. A prickling at the base of my spine and a lightening of the pressure on my chest. They were still with me, the winter ghosts, but they were retreating into the wings.

'Fabrissa?'

I raised my head and looked straight ahead. The briefest sensation, no more than the tremor of a butterfly's wing. A moment, not of enlightenment, but of grace in a twist of tumbling black hair and a pale face. I scrambled to my feet and took a hesitant step forward. The vision slipped instantly away, perishing, falling, no sooner seen than gone.

'No.' My cry rang out around the cave. 'Stay.'

I clenched my left hand into a fist, feeling my broken fingernails digging into my scratched palm. I tried to remember the feel of her, so light, the touch of her, her bright grey eyes and the laughter lines at the corners of her mouth.

I took another step closer to where she had been. The weakening beam of light picked out a fragment of blue lying on the ground. A deep blue, the colour of my brother's eyes, of flax blossom in the Sussex fields in June. The exact colour of the dress Fabrissa had worn. I could see clearly, too clearly, threads of yellow where the cross had been.

I knelt down beside her, more than anything wanting to feel the frail white skin beneath my fingers. But there was only the hardness of bone beneath my hand. I tried to speak her name, to bring her back to life, but I could not.

My ribs seemed to tighten, to crack. Then, at last, I heard her, dazzling in the darkness, speaking to me and me alone.

'*Freddie . . .*'

'I'm here,' I said, half weeping, half laughing. I knew she could hear me. 'I kept my word. I came to find you.'

Did I hold her to me then? I cannot have done, for I knew she was shadow and dust. And yet, I have the memory that, for an instant, I felt her warm in my arms and that I sighed. I had come for her and so she had returned to me. Come to take me home.

I could feel myself slipping further into the darkness, but now I welcomed it. And she started to talk, finishing the story she had begun. I laid my head in her lap, I am sure of it, as I listened, entranced once more, by the beautiful rise and fall of her voice telling the end of her tale of the mountains and the ghosts that dwelt within them.

My eyes slowly closed, lulled by the rhythm of her words, until finally all was silence. And in that silence she slipped away. I felt her go. I cried out, but her ghost, spirit, emanation, whatever it was – whatever she was – was gone. And this time, I knew she would not return.

I was slipping further into unconsciousness. I did not wish to wake. As the light dimmed and dimmed again, I thought of the lights going down in the auditorium and the hush of that Christmas Eve in the Lyric Theatre. I thought of Neverland and Pan. Of George and me eating jellies and giggling. Of how we were both wiser now and knew dying never was an awfully big adventure. And then I was smiling to think that I might see George again, and Fabrissa, and that that would be all right.

Then, suddenly, I was struggling. I couldn't join them, not yet. The thought was as sharp as a splinter under my skin. Although I had found her, I had not brought her home. Just as I had never brought George home.

'Fabrissa . . .'

But the word died on my lips. I was floating down through the darkness, lower into the ice floes of the Antarctic, into the impenetrable silence. The silence of the end of days.

The Hospital in Foix

White faces, white walls, white sheets on the bed.

When I came round, I was in the hospital in Foix. I wasn't sure what day it was, nor how long I had been in the hospital, nor how I came to be there. I had been unconscious for two days, they told me. The fever I'd so foolishly thought to have shrugged off had returned with a vengeance, brought on by the exertions of the climb and hypothermia. For a while, my life hung in the balance.

For forty-eight hours, I drifted in and out of consciousness. Time had little meaning. How could it, after what had happened in Nulle? Now, then, in the past, in the present, all just words. The passing of days, as measured by the accretion of seconds and minutes and hours, was too rigid.

Madame Galy made the journey down the valley of the Vicdessos to sit with me. Though unconscious,

I was aware of her gentle presence, her soothing hand on my brow. And in the seclusion and privacy of the night, when she did not think I could hear, she whispered of her son who had gone to war, like George, and never come back. Of his name, Augustin Pierre Galy, carved with those of his friends on the memorial in the corner of the place de l'Église. When the fever had worn itself out and finally I woke up, she was no longer there.

At first, I couldn't remember what had happened or how I had come to be there. I looked down and saw my hands were bandaged and felt pressure on my temples. I realised I had a dressing on my head, too tight for comfort, and my throat was sore. As if I had been shouting. Or possibly even crying.

Little by little, my memories started to surface. I tried to piece together the sequence of events, all of it, from the point at which the car went off the road. There had been a storm and I had crashed, that wasn't in doubt. Nor that I had found my way to Nulle and Fabrissa. But everything from that point became blurred, indistinct.

I did remember climbing up into the cave and dismantling the prison wall with my bare hands. I remembered chancing upon the letter, then making my way through the narrow gap that led to the inner cave. Then finding the skeletons of those with whom I had spent an evening. The winter ghosts, as Breillac called them, long dead. I remembered Fabrissa. And my eyes filled with tears.

Later, when I was a little stronger, I learned the doctors had been mystified by how ill I was. The fever had been aggressive and my body temperature in the cave had dropped to perilously low levels, but at the same time there was no severe injury that accounted for my disorientation. The abrasions on my hands and face were minor, and though I appeared to have knocked my head, it was nothing serious. Only one nurse understood, a pretty dark girl from Nulle originally, with round kitten eyes. She knew I had ventured too close to the grave and had been tainted by it. Death had slipped into my bones.

Medical men came and went. Doctors, psychiatrists, the ward sister and her flock of starched nurses in squeaking, rubber-soled shoes. On the surface, it seemed that history was repeating itself. A sanatorium in Sussex, a hospital in Foix, a patient unable to cope. But I was not the same man. For though they poked and prodded at me, I felt clear in my mind. I was no longer doped up, just tired.

And the knowledge that I had done what had been asked of me sustained me. I had found Fabrissa.

With each passing hour, more memories returned. Fragments of the days leading up to this point, filling in the gaps like missing pieces in a jigsaw puzzle. My room in the boarding house, the crunch of sparkling ice underfoot in the place de l'Église when I set out for the Ostal. Watching the pale sun light the valley at dawn.

Fabrissa at my side.

On 22 December, my friends came from Ax-les-Thermes. Having received my letter, they had waited for me to get in touch. When after four days there was still no word, they made enquiries with Madame Galy and found out I was laid up in hospital.

They stayed for a couple of hours. From them, I learned my discovery in the cave was something of a coup. *La Dépêche*, the local newspaper, had devoted a whole page to the story. Of course it was early days and on account of the season, there was difficulty getting hold of the top men from Toulouse – archaeologists, pathologists, battalions of experts – but the consensus was that the skeletons were some six hundred years old. The cache of grave goods, pots and domestic artefacts, all confirmed that.

I understood a little more. Not a tragedy in living memory, but a story far older.

According to the experts quoted in the newspaper, the bodies were most likely to be traced back to the wars of religion in the early fourteenth century. Local historians had recorded similar incidents when members of the last remaining Cathar communities in the region had been trapped inside the caves in which they had taken shelter. In Lombrives, for example. No one had known there might be another similar site so close.

'Breillac knew,' I murmured to myself.

The whole village knew. My pretty nurse, Madame and Monsieur Galy, all of them had grown up in the shadow of the deep sadness that enveloped the village. Not only from the last war, but all the wars going back through the centuries. The inhabitants of Nulle, present and past, knew how such profound grief erodes the spirit.

But as I listened to my friends talk, and heard the excitement in their voice at being caught up, at one remove, in such an historic mystery, relief seeped through me. For although it was not I who physically carried her body home, my exploration of the cave had set in motion the reclaiming of those lost so many years ago. Now the real work of identification and burial could begin.

My thoughts drifted back to Fabrissa. She had led me there, hadn't she? A flash of blue against the white of the mountains? And I had, for a perfect, impossible moment, surely held her in my arms.

*

I had no other visitors until Christmas Eve.

As the evening shadows were falling across the neat rows of beds and the nurses were lighting the lamps in the ward, a figure appeared in the doorway. Broad shoulders, awkward in the sterile atmosphere.

'Guillaume, come in.'

I was genuinely delighted to see him. He approached the bed cautiously, clutching his cap in his broad red hands, giving the impression he was regretting his decision to visit. He had something to say to me, he said, something that had been bothering him. It wouldn't take long.

'Take a seat.'

I tried to sit up, too fast it seemed, for the motion made my head spin and I slumped back on the pillows.

'Should I fetch someone?'

'No, no,' I said. 'Got to take it slower, that's all.'

He perched awkwardly on the edge of the chair.

'You had something to tell me?' I prompted.

He nodded, but he could not meet my eye and didn't seem to know how to start. In the end, I decided to help him out.

'How long were you gone?'

Having a straightforward question to answer helped Guillaume get into his stride. It had taken three hours, he said. When they returned to the car with the truck from Tarascon, they found me gone. His father and Pierre were all for thinking I'd returned to Nulle, and concentrated on the car. But he, remembering the questions I had asked, wasn't so sure. He couldn't dismiss from his mind how I'd kept looking across the valley and asked questions about escarpment and caves. The longer he thought about it, the more sure he became that I had gone to investigate.

Against the wishes of his father, Guillaume persuaded the mechanic to drive on to Miglos rather than return to Tarascon. He climbed down from the road to the plateau and saw footprints on the mountain path. Given the lateness of the hour and the temperature, which was now little above freezing, he was certain they were mine.

'But once I was down there, monsieur, it wasn't clear where you had gone after that. The ground was too hard, ice not earth, so no tracks. And there were many routes you might have taken.

'I could hear my brother calling me from the road. They were all impatient, certain it was a wild goose chase. I admit I was starting to doubt, too. The light was fading. I knew it was unwise to carry on searching. But I also knew that, if you had not returned to Nulle, you would not survive the night out there alone. Then I saw . . .'

Guillaume stopped, his cheeks red.

'What, Guillaume?' I said urgently. 'What did you see?'

'I don't rightly know, monsieur. Someone. I swear to you, on my life, I saw someone waving to attract my attention.'

My heart skipped a beat. 'A woman?'

He shook his head. 'I wasn't sure. I was too far away. All I saw was a flash of blue, a long blue coat. I thought it could be you, monsieur, if you had changed your clothes at your motorcar before setting out.'

'It wasn't me.'

'No?'

'No.'

Guillaume held my gaze for a moment, his honest eyes flickering with doubt, then he looked away.

'I climbed up to the place you . . . the figure . . . had been, but there was no one there. I didn't know what to make of it. Then I saw, not footprints exactly, but marks on the ground, leading towards the cliff face. When I took a closer look, I saw the opening into the cave hidden beneath the escarpment.'

'It's lucky for me that you did, Guillaume,' I said quietly.

'I called up to my father and Pierre, who—'

'They could see you?'

'No, they were too far away. And by now it was nearly dark. But they could hear me. It was very cold, very still. The noise carries in winter when only the evergreens are in leaf.'

'Yes, I see.'

'I found the rubble in the passageway where you had broken down the wall, then followed you down into the cave, then the cavern beyond.' He stopped. 'My father always said, but . . .' He licked his dry lips. 'I had to think about you, monsieur, how to get you out and to a doctor. You were unconscious, barely

breathing. I couldn't think of the others. Not then.'
He met my gaze. 'And you are sure it could not have
been you that I saw?'

'Quite sure.'

'It's just that . . . you were lying there covered in a
blue cloak. It was odd, the exact match to the dress of
the . . . the body of a woman. Dressed in a long blue
robe, the same colour as . . . You were lying beside
her.' He hesitated. 'The same blue I . . . the person
waving to me.'

I realised that was the crux of it. Guillaume did
not want to believe his father's superstitious tales
were true and I did not blame him for that.

'Probably just a trick of the light,' I said.

Guillaume nodded. I had not reassured him, but
he was grateful the matter was settled and would not
be talked of again. He fished in his pocket.

'And there was this, monsieur,' he said.

He held out to me the sheet of parchment I'd
picked up in the cave, then forgotten about in the
horror of discovering the mass grave.

'You were holding on to it so tightly, I thought it
must be important.'

He leaned forward and put it on the bed beside me. The
coarse weave was yellow against the white, white sheets.

Gratitude flooded through me. 'Thank you. From the bottom of my heart, thank you.' I picked it up. 'Did you read it?'

He shook his head. 'It's in the old language.'

'Occitan, but surely . . .' I stopped, realising he might not be able to read. I had no wish to embarrass him. 'If you hadn't stuck with it, Guillaume, well . . . I owe you my life.'

And you, Fabrissa, I added under my breath. And you . . .

'Anyone would have done the same,' he said gruffly, standing up. The feet of the chair scraped on the linoleum. He was not a man to make anything of his own heroism, and now he had discharged his duty he was eager to leave.

I knew he was wrong. Although George told me of the towering acts of courage he had witnessed, not every man had it in him to put his life on the line for another.

'Better get off,' he said.

'It was good of you to come. If there's anything you need, any way I can thank you for—'

'No,' he said quickly. 'My father said to pass on our thanks to you. He said he thought you would know what he meant.'

[237]

I hesitated, then nodded. 'I think I do,' I said. 'Give my regards to him. And to Madame Galy.'

'I will.'

He put his cap back on his head and turned to go.

'Merry Christmas to you, Guillaume.'

'And to you, monsieur.'

He lingered for a moment, his broad frame filling the doorway and blotting out the light from the corridor beyond. Then he was gone.

I held the parchment close to my face, too nervous to open it even though I knew I would not be able to read it. But I knew it was meant for me. A letter from Fabrissa to me. No, not me. Whoever it was that heard the voices in the mountain and came to bring them home.

I opened it flat. The handwriting was scratched and uneven, lines overlapping one another as if the author had run out of ink or light or strength. I still couldn't distinguish one word from the next, but this time my tired eyes found a date at the bottom of the page and three initials: FDN.

Was 'F' for Fabrissa? I wanted to believe so, certainly. But as to the rest? It would have to wait. I would have to wait.

I lay back on the pillows.

There was no rational way to explain any of it. Only that it had happened. For a moment, I had slipped between the cracks in time and Fabrissa had come to me. A ghost, a spirit? Or a real woman displaced from her own time to that cold December? It was beyond my comprehension, but now I understood it did not matter. Only the consequences mattered. She had sought my help and I had given it.

'My own love,' I said.

Because of her, I had faced my own demons. She had freed me to look to the future. Not endlessly trapped in that one moment when the clocks stopped on 15 September 1916. Not stuck on 11 November 1921 at the memorial to the Royal Sussex Regiment in Chichester Cathedral, unable to bear, for one second longer, not knowing where George had fallen. Not condemned to watch champagne spill and drip, drip from the table of an expensive restaurant in Piccadilly.

I closed my eyes. Around me, the noise of the hospital. The squeak of wheels in a distant corridor. And somewhere, out of sight, the sound of voices singing carols for Christmas.

TOULOUSE

April 1933

Return to La Rue des Pénitents Gris

'And so,' Freddie said, 'here I am. I had not been able to come before.'

He sat back in his chair, his hand cupped around the tumbler of brandy. Saurat looked at him.

The shadows had lengthened while they had talked. The late-afternoon sun, shining through the metal grille across the window of the bookshop, cast diamond-shaped patterns on the floor inside the bookshop.

Saurat cleared this throat. 'And for the past five years?'

'I returned to England. Not straight away, but when it was clear there was nothing . . .' Freddie broke off. 'Then, of course, the Slump, and all that followed. My few stocks and shares became worthless overnight. I had no option but to find a way of earning a living. I rented rooms in a house and got myself a job with the Imperial War Graves Commission in London. Modest enough, but sufficient for my needs.'

'I see.'

'We unveiled the memorial at Thiepval, to those who died at the Battle of the Somme, on the first of July nineteen thirty-two. My brother's regiment, the three Southdowner Battalions, went over the top on the eve of the Somme. They took the German front line and held it for a while, but then fell back. In less than five hours, seventeen officers and nearly three hundred and fifty men of Sussex were lost. The following day, the main engagement began.'

'And since then?'

'Travelling, around France and Belgium for the most part. I'm one of the team of men responsible for the upkeep of the headstones and the crosses of sacrifice and the cemeteries.'

'So no one is forgotten.'

'We remember so that such slaughter is never allowed to happen again. George, Madame Galy's son, the men of the Ariège, the Southdowners, we must remember them. All the lost boys.' Freddie stopped. This was not the time or the place.

He took a sip of his drink, then carefully replaced the heavy tumbler on the table and pushed the parchment across the green felt.

Saurat held Freddie's gaze for a moment. In his eyes, he saw neither expectation nor anxiety, but instead resolve. He realised that, whatever lay within the letter, it would come as no surprise to the Englishman.

'You are ready?'

Freddie closed his eyes. 'I am.'

Saurat adjusted his spectacles on the bridge of his nose, then began to read.

'Bones and shadows and dust. I am the last.

The others have slipped away into darkness. Around me now, at the end of my days, only an echo in the still air of the memory of those who once I loved.

Solitude, silence. Peyre sant.

The end is coming and I welcome it as one might a familiar friend, long absent. This has been a slow death, trapped here. One by one, every heart stopped beating. My brother first, then my mother and my father. Now the only sound is my shallow breathing. That, and the gentle dripping of water down the mossy walls of the cave. As if the mountain itself is weeping. As if it, too, is mourning the dead.

We heard them, their footsteps, and thought ourselves safe. We heard the rocks, one by one, being piled up, the hammering of the wood, but still we did not understand that they were sealing the entrance to the cave for good. And this underground city, lit only by candles and torches, once our refuge, became our tomb.

These are the last words I will write. It will not be long. My body does not obey me now. My last candle is burning out. This is my testament, the record of how once men and women and children lived and died in this forgotten corner of the world. I write it down so that those who come after us will know the truth.

I do not fear death. But I fear the forgetting. I fear that there will be no one to mark the moment of our passing. One day, someone will find us. Find us and bring us home. For when all else is done, only words remain. Words endure.

And I shall set this last truth down. We are who we are because of those we choose to love and because of those who love us. Peyre-sant, God of good spirits, have mercy on my soul.

Prima
In the year of our Lord, thirteen twenty-nine'

'Someone will find us,' repeated Freddie.

Saurat peered at him over the top of his half-moon spectacles. He waited a while as the words echoed into the silence of the books on the shelves of the narrow little shop.

'Spring thirteen twenty-nine,' he said in the end.

Freddie opened his eyes. 'Yes.'

'More than six hundred years ago.'

'Yes.'

The two men looked at one another. Only the ticking of the clock and the motes of dust dancing in the slatted afternoon light marked that time moved at all.

'Have you been back to Nulle?' Saurat asked.

'I have. On several occasions.'

'And?'

Freddie smiled. 'It is different. A place restored to itself. Monsieur and Madame Galy are still there and their little boarding house is thriving.'

'No longer living in the shadows.'

'Not at all. Nulle itself has become quite a centre for walking holidays in the mountains south of Tarascon. Guillaume Breillac makes a good living at it. There's even talk of building a funicular railway to take visitors up to the caves.'

'A tourist destination.'

'In a modest way. It doesn't yet rival Lombrives or Niaux, but perhaps one day it will.'

Freddie looked towards the sunlit window and wondered, as he had not been able to stop himself doing many times in the past few years, what Fabrissa would say could she see the village come back to life again.

'Certainly, the facts of the story are accurate,' Saurat said. 'In the beginning of the fourteenth century, the remaining Cathar communities were hunted down and eliminated. At Lombrives, more than five hundred were found by the soldiers of the Comte de Foix-Sabarthès, the future Henri IV, two hundred and fifty years after they had been entombed in the caves there.'

Freddie nodded. 'I read of it.'

'And those you met in the Ostal – Guillaume Marty, Na Azéma, the Maury sisters, Authier – all typical Cathar names of the period. Fabrissa also.'

'Yes.'

Saurat hesitated. 'Still, I am not certain what you think actually happened that night.'

Freddie held his gaze. 'We are modern men, Saurat. We live in an age of science and rational thought.

And even if it has not done us any good, we are not obliged to live, as our forebears did, under the oppressive and superstitious shadow of religion, of irrationality, of demons and retributive spirits. We know how psychology can account for night terrors, for hallucinations, for voices in the dark. We are aware of the tricks our minds can play on us, on our delicate, vulnerable, suggestible, shabby little minds.' He shrugged. 'I lose count of how many times I was told that when I was ill.'

'You are saying the doctors are right?'

Freddie smiled. 'They may be right, Saurat, but I know she was there. Fabrissa was there. I saw her. I talked to her, I held her in my arms. While I was in Nulle, tramping the grieving land that surrounded the village, she was as real to me as you are sitting here.'

'And now?'

At first, Freddie did not answer. 'There are moments of intense emotion – love, death, grief – where we may slip between the cracks. Then, I believe that time can stretch or contract or collide in ways science cannot account for. Perhaps this is what happened when I smashed the car and knocked myself out, perhaps not.' He shrugged. 'That such a person as

Fabrissa once lived in the village of Nulle, I do not doubt. That somehow she sought me out, I also do not doubt.'

'Faith, then?' said Saurat, looking around at the book-lined shelves. 'A belief in something more than this?'

'Who's to say? Life is not, as we are taught, a matter of seeking answers, but rather learning which are the questions we should ask.'

Saurat looked down at the antique letter, at the words he had so painstakingly translated for his English visitor.

'Why did you wait so long?'

'I needed to be ready to hear it.'

'Ah.'

'And to make an end of things.'

Saurat put his glasses down on the table and rubbed his eyes.

'Perhaps also, because you knew what it would say? I had the impression nothing in it surprised you.'

Freddie shrugged again. '"We are who we are, because of those we choose to love and because of those who love us." That's what Fabrissa wrote.' He smiled. 'One does not need a translator to understand the truth of those words.'

Both men fell silent. Inside the bookshop, the clock continued to mark the passing of the day. In the street outside, the burst of a car horn, a woman calling to a child or a lover in an affectionate voice, the sounds of the modern city on an afternoon in spring.

'What do you intend to do with the letter?' Saurat asked after a while.

'Nothing.'

'I'd give you a fair price.'

Freddie laughed. 'I don't think it's possible to put a price on such a thing. Do you?'

'Perhaps not,' Saurat conceded. 'But if you should ever change your mind . . . '

'Of course, I'll bear you in mind.'

Freddie stood up. He put on his overcoat, slipped the letter into the pasteboard wallet.

'You'll allow me to pay you for your time?'

Saurat held up his hands. 'The pleasure was mine.'

Freddie pulled out a fifty-franc note all the same and laid it on the counter.

'To donate to a good cause, then,' he said.

Saurat acknowledged the gift with a nod. He did not pick it up, but neither did he attempt to give it back.

At the door, the two men shook hands, on the afternoon, on the story, on the secret they now shared.

'And what of your brother?' Saurat said. 'In your travels, your work for the War Graves Commission, did you ever find the answer to the question you were seeking? Did you find out what happened to him?'

Freddie put on his trilby and slipped his hands into his fawn gloves. 'He is known unto God,' he said. 'That is enough.'

Then he turned and walked back up the rue des Pénitents Gris, his shadow striding before him.

Acknowledgements

I am very grateful to all those who have worked so hard on *The Winter Ghosts*.

My agent, Mark Lucas, continues to be an inspiration, a wonderful editor, and makes it fun despite the absence of Post-it notes! To Mark, Alice Saunders, and everyone at LAW, thank you.

At Orion, a huge thank you to everyone in the editorial, publicity, marketing, sales and art departments, especially the editorial dream-team of Jon Wood and Genevieve Pegg, as well as Malcolm Edwards, Lisa Milton, Susan Lamb, Jo Carpenter, Lucie Stericker, Mark Rusher, Gaby Young and Helen Ewing; and to Brian Gallagher for the beautiful illustrations.

I would not have finished the book without the affection and practical help of family and friends, especially my mother-in-law, Rosie Turner; my parents, Richard and Barbara Mosse; fellow dog-walkers, Cath O'Hanlon, Patrick O'Hanlon and Julie Pembery and my sister, Caroline Matthews; Amanda Ross, Jon Evans, Lucinda Montefiore, Tessa Ross, Robert Dye, Maria Rejt, Peter Clayton, Rachel Holmes, Bob Pulley and Mari Pulley.

Finally, without the love and support of my husband Greg Mosse, and our children Martha and Felix, none of this would matter. It is to them, as always, that the book is dedicated.

Author's Note

By 1328, the medieval Christian heresy now referred to as Catharism had been all but destroyed. After the fall of Montségur in 1244 and the fortress of Quéribus in 1255, the remaining Cathars were driven back into the high valleys of the Pyrenees. Many Cathar priests – *parfaits* and *parfaites* – were executed, or driven into Lombardy or Spain.

Despite this, the early fourteenth-century saw a remarkable renaissance of Cathar communities in the upper Ariège, principally around Tarascon and Ax-les-Thermes (then known as Ax) and key villages, such as Montaillou. The Inquisitional Courts in Pamiers (for the Ariège) and Carcassonne (for the Languedoc) continued to persecute and hunt down the heretics (as they were considered). Those taken were imprisoned in dungeons known as Murs. Principal in this was Jacques Fournier, a Cistercian monk, who rose quickly through the Catholic ranks, becoming bishop of Pamiers in 1317, of Mirepoix in 1326, a cardinal in 1327, and, finally, Pope in Avignon in 1334, as Benedict XII. It is an irony that Fournier's Inquisition Register, detailing all interrogations and depositions made to the courts on his watch, is one of the most important surviving historical records about Cathar experience in fourteenth-century Languedoc. The last Cathar *parfait*, Guillaume Bélibaste, was burnt at the stake in 1321.

During the vicious final years of the extermination of the Cathars, whole villages were arrested – such as at Montaillou in the spring and autumn of 1308. There is evidence that entire communities took refuge in the labyrinth network of caves of the Haute Vallée of the Pyrenees, the most infamous example being in the caves of Lombrives, just south of Tarascon-sur-Ariège. Hunted down by the soldiers in the spring of 1328, hundreds of men, women and children fled into the caves. The soldiers of the Inquisition realised that, rather than continue to play cat-and-mouse, they could use traditional siege tactics and block the entrance, bringing the game to an end. This they did, entombing everyone inside in some kind of medieval Masada.

It was only 250 years later, when the troops of the Count of Foix-Sabarthès, the man who was to become King Henry IV of France, excavated the caves that the tragedy was revealed. Whole families were discovered – their skeletons lying side by side, bones fused together, their last precious objects beside them – and finally brought down from the stone refuge that had become a living tomb.

It is this grisly fragment of Cathar history that was the inspiration for *The Winter Ghosts*.* The village of Nulle does not exist.

For those readers who want to know more about the final days of Catharism, Emmanuel Le Roy Ladurie's classic *Montaillou*, first published in 1978, is the most complete and detailed explanation of the complications of life, faith and tradition in fourteenth-century Ariège. *De l'Héritage des Cathares* (available in translation as *The Inheritance of the Cathars*) by the French mystic and Tarasconais Cathar historian of the 1930s and 1940s, Antonin Gadal, is well worth dipping into. René Weis' *The Yellow Cross: The Story of the Last Cathars 1290–1329*, Anne Brenon's *Pèire Authier: Le Dernier des Cathares* and Greg Mosse's *Secrets of the Labyrinth* are all excellent.

Kate Mosse
Toulouse, April 2009

* An earlier version of this story was published as *The Cave*, a novella written for the 2009 Quick Reads initiative aimed at adult emergent readers.